Marry Me, Marla

A Wild Rose Ridge Top Story

Mary A. Felkins

Gardenia PRESS

Ebook ASIN: B0DXXBGZ9K

Print ISBN: 979-8-9862201-9-2

Great effort is put into ensuring accuracy when representing the characters in their professions. Any errors are due to author misunderstanding during research.

Scripture

I have chosen you and have not rejected you. So do not fear, for I am with you. Do not be dismayed, for I am your God.

I will strengthen you and help you.

I will uphold you with my righteous right hand.

—Isaiah 41:9-10

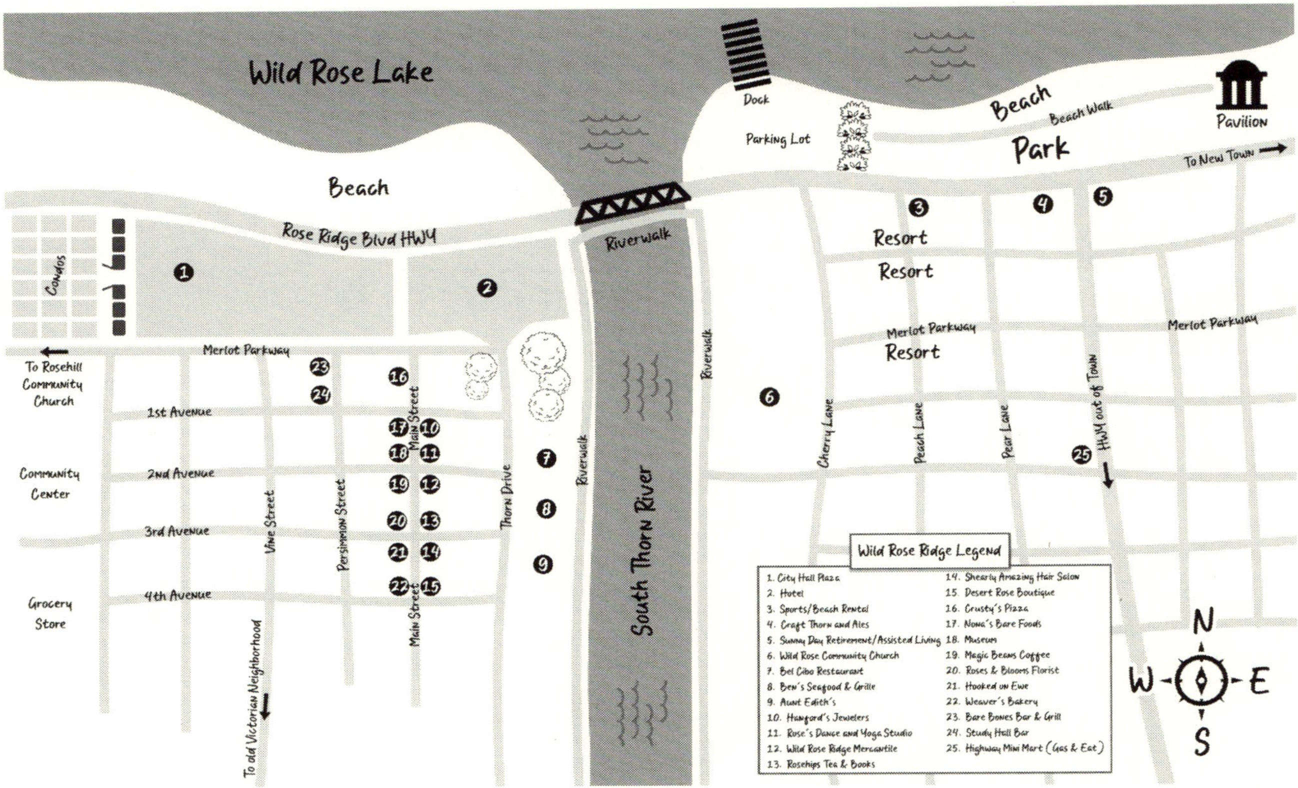

Wild Rose Lake
Dock
Beach
Beach Walk
Pavilion
Parking Lot
Park
To New Town
Beach
Rose Ridge Blvd HWY
Riverwalk
Condos
Resort
Resort
Merlot Parkway
Resort
Merlot Parkway
Merlot Parkway
To Rosehill Community Church
1st Avenue
Community Center
2nd Avenue
3rd Avenue
Grocery Store
4th Avenue
Vine Street
Persimmon Street
Main Street
Main Street
Thorn Drive
Riverwalk
South Thorn River
Riverwalk
Cherry Lane
Peach Lane
Pear Lane
HWY out of Town
To old Victorian Neighborhood
Wild Rose Ridge Legend
1. City Hall Plaza
2. Hotel
3. Sports/Beach Rental
4. Craft Thorn and Ales
5. Sunny Day Retirement/Assisted Living
6. Wild Rose Community Church
7. Bel Cibo Restaurant
8. Ben's Seafood & Grille
9. Aunt Edith's
10. Hanford's Jewelers
11. Rose's Dance and Yoga Studio
12. Wild Rose Ridge Mercantile
13. Rosehips Tea & Books
14. Shearly Amazing Hair Salon
15. Desert Rose Boutique
16. Crusty's Pizza
17. Nona's Bare Foods
18. Museum
19. Magic Beans Coffee
20. Roses & Blooms Florist
21. Hooked on Ewe
22. Weaver's Bakery
23. Bare Bones Bar & Grill
24. Study Hall Bar
25. Highway Mini Mart (Gas & Eat)
N
W
E
S

Chapter One

A real hero for Marla Mavis was out there—she just knew it, even if she had to dream him up. As a small town romance columnist, that might be her specialty. But oh, how it played cruel games with her heart.

Marla navigated through the maze of cubicles on her way to her private office at the *Wild Rose Observer,* a central Washington small town newspaper. She stopped at Angela Tambo's desk a stapler's throw away and brought a hand to her hip.

"Word is circulating that my column is nothing but fluff. Shallow, forgettable content."

Angela spun in her chair. "Fluff sells and pays the bills."

Marla returned a scowl to singe Angela's hair off her scalp. "I'm done writing only for a paycheck."

A paycheck that enabled Marla to publish happy endings, a jarring reminder she had yet to find her own.

Not everyone—including her ex-fiancé—was willing to overlook scarred parts.

Hot off the press, Monday's edition of the *Observer* lay on Angela's desk. Marla rolled the newspaper and brandished it in a battle cry. "I fought too hard last year to defeat breast cancer to be viewed as a superficial writer. I want to appeal to the masses and publish relatable, poignant stories that will ping with readers. It's time I rebranded myself and left a memorable legacy."

Angela returned a derisive 'legacy for who?' expression, then said, "Why don't you interview the couples in town who've married over the past two years and publish a 'How are they doing now?' article."

And be reminded that Marla wasn't—and might not ever be—among them? Forget it! It was hard enough on her heart that she collaborated with local matchmakers to covertly establish perfect pairings between unsuspecting couples in town and had cornered herself into publishing those romantic stories.

Marla left Angela to her work and strode with a coveted travel tumbler of coffee, past the jigsaw of cubicles, down the hallway to her office. She gave her potted Chroma Belize Rubber Plant near the door a spritz.

Through the frame of an ample window, the dismal winter landscape clung to the fragile but determined beginnings of spring.

Her heart leapt at a beguiling bouquet on her desk. She sniffed at the white hydrangeas and satiny red roses. Natural light played on the dewy petals.

Did Marla's ex finally realize what he gave up? Was this his way of winning her back? While everything in her reared at the idea of giving him another chance, he was an otherwise admirable, successful guy. It wouldn't be altogether crazy to give him the opportunity to elaborate on the reasons for breaking off their engagement after her cancer diagnosis.

She plucked the card off the holder. "To my one and only Lorraine, Happy 35th anniversary to the best wife a man could have. Forever yours, Phil."

From the open doorway, Lorraine Schulte, a seasoned mother *and happily married* woman of three adult children, drew her gaze over the rim of her reading glasses. "I've been dying to know. Who's your prince charmer?"

A raggedy sigh breezed out. "Phil. Your husband."

Lorraine's mouth popped open.

Marla handed the card to Lorraine who peered at it.

An awkward smile drew at her mouth. "Guess the delivery guy at Roses 'n Blooms made a mistake."

A brutal mistake. "At my expense."

"Sorry, sugar."

Swallowing past a boulder, Marla sat and awakened her keyboard.

The heady floral fragrance intensified. Marla moved the bouquet aside, nearly upsetting her coffee. "You know I despise pity. Anyway, the right man would know not to send flowers."

"What woman doesn't love flowers?"

"One who isn't wooed by them."

Lorraine perched on the edge of Marla's desk. "I've been your line editor here for years, and I'm not sure if you even know what would turn your head."

A wholly devoted 'till death do us part' love. Nothing Marla or her single mom had experienced.

"I know I don't want a proposal. Not another one, anyway."

"And I don't want a spacious vacation home in the French Riviera where Phil and I can enjoy Mediterranean sunsets," Lorraine smarted.

Marla stood to relocate the hefty vase to a side table between two repurposed armchairs. She turned and smacked the window with her rebuttal. "Where was my ex during my chemotherapy, radiation, or surgery?"

"He had already called off the engagement at that point, and you chose to receive treatments out of town. How was *anyone* supposed to be there?"

Marla's breath fogged the glass. "Someone *was* there."

"Who?"

"I don't know."

Lorraine clucked her tongue.

"Seriously. I felt a presence," Marla said.

That same fleeting, but strikingly familiar sensation rushed through her limbs. She put a hand near her heart. "After the presence weakened, I would discover a gift or a card left somewhere in the room."

The wall doubled as a screen where Marla projected the vision, a mystery man who appeared in her imagination. The skies were idyllically clear and warm. Something familiar hovered in his eyes.

Had they met?

He was remarkably lean, tall, and handsome. His posture conveyed an openness and his gaze oozed kindness. Acceptance … pleasuring in her.

This beautiful make-believe creature appeared in her fantasies as a vessel of healing. Born of heaven, he saw her scars and didn't recoil. Rather, he opened his arms to her—

Snap, snap. "You're daydreaming again."

Poof! The vision evaporated, though they had occurred with greater frequency over the last few weeks as though she'd been the subject of a lover's spell that cast a pixie dust of happily ever after promises.

But cancer had taught Marla what it felt like to want what she could never have. According to her therapist, fantasizing impossible realities was how her mind coped with the trauma of loss.

"No one around the office appreciates an over-caffeinated Marla Mavis, but sugar, you need a refill."

Marla ignored Lorraine's comment, felt around in her desk drawer, and slipped out one of the precious cards. She cleared her throat as though addressing the Senate. "You are not alone, Marla. I'm fighting with and for you."

Shivering in the ripple effect of Lorraine's thunder-struck expression, Marla returned the card and slid the drawer shut with her hip.

Intrigue lifted Lorraine's brow.

"I received several anonymous cards throughout my treatments, urging me to stay in the fight."

"Take them to a forensic documents expert."

"I've already considered that, but I'd need an exemplary sample for comparison." She paused to muse, then said, "When I received a No Evidence of Disease medical clearance, the mysterious gift-giver left me a custom T-shirt that reads, 'I'm Marla, a cancer survivor. What's your super power?'"

Lorraine drew clasped hands to her neck. "It's finally your time."

"It's your time, all right." That from the news director,

Cecilia Dilly—or Cilly Dilly, as Marla had privately named her.

Cecilia claimed the turquoise mid-century style chair at Marla's desk. She tented her hands on her knee. Her salty auburn updo, small nose, black eyes, and white blouse with cuffed high neck delivered the look of a spinster—a horrid picture of what might be Marla's fate.

"I need you to do a general news story on the Arrington Kissing Arch for next Friday's column. Include a list of the couples who have wed there."

Marla fit a smile to her lips in restrained protest. "I'm already facing a hard deadline for the quarterly report on Wild Rose Ridge's most swoon-worthy couples." An article Marla had been procrastinating.

Cilly's tiny chin drew taut. "I've assigned the quarterly to Glen Conklin. You'll retain the by-line."

A former Harvard Professor of Ancient and Classic History? This would never do!

"Glen's writing voice is flat and unfeeling. It smacks of dry, rote academia. My column is known for sparks of romance. I refuse to be misrepresented."

Marla's haughty comeback might be costly, but she saw no wisdom in a man ghost-writing her column.

"I've informed Glen that you are to sign off on it." Cilly wiggled her fingers. "Sprinkle in all the sizzle and sass you please."

"I'll be up all night."

"Indeed. The hallmark of a good journalist." Cilly commenced pacing and drew her hands behind her lower back. "If you do this right, readers will forget the impact of last week's column."

Sure, Marla needed a shot at redemption for inadvertently publishing false information that resulted in a high-profile member of city council breaking off his engagement.

But wasn't there something unethical about coercion?

"Cilly, er, Cecilia, last year's harrowing health scare gave me a new outlook on life. I want to write something meaningful and memorable."

"Pah. No one will take you seriously."

"It's time they did. Cancer is no joke."

"No, of course not, but—"

"I'd like to up my game, raise the bar of substance."

Cilly paused her pacing long enough to give Marla a contemplative, thin-lipped smile. "Very well."

"Thank you."

"As you know, the Observer celebrates its 50th anniversary this year. In conjunction with the state-wide emphasis on benevolent communities, we have been nominated for the Hazel Fowler Wingate National Award for excellence in small town journalism. The exposure will boost our economy and drive attention to Mayor Weaver's campaign to increase charitable giving."

Lorraine wedged herself into the conversation. "I heard that the Rose of Sharon Rescue Mission is struggling to stay afloat. Its new director could use a boost."

"Nice angle," Cilly said. She slid Lorraine a side-eye that smacked of conspiracy before returning her gaze to Marla. "I need your undivided attention on this. Top-notch reporting."

"You got it."

Cilly chopped at her palm with the side of her hand. "You'll have a hard deadline of three weeks' time. I want vivid detail, names, photos. Lorraine will proof your content before it comes to my inbox for approval."

The urge to puff her chest and salute nearly cast propriety to the wind.

Cilly's gaze shrank to pebbles. She pressed the heels of her therapeutic soles together like a Russian ballerina. "Do not disappoint me—or the town."

In order for Marla to re-brand her image, this post would have to be her finest to date. Thorough research was paramount. No detail could be overlooked, no matter how seemingly insignificant.

According to the Rose of Sharon website—woefully outdated and difficult to navigate—the director was a widower in his 60's. But Marla knew better. She'd written about the director's marriage and swift relocation with his wife to her hometown in sunny Florida.

Apparently, finding true love did not bode well for the Rose of Sharon nor the people who'd depended on it.

Marla added the scant online data to her notes app and documented the address.

Stepping onto the pavement outside the *Observer*, a brisk wind funneled from the ridgeline and slicked past storefronts. Hanging planters flourished with greenery along the line of fluted gas lanterns.

The *Observer* was proudly housed at the northwest corner of 2nd Avenue and Persimmon Street in the original three-story building erected in Old Town in the early 1900's.

The iconic brick façade of the upper levels matched the style of several retailers on Main Street a block east. Soothing vintage green paint colored the main level. Bronze lettering above the entrance identified the enviable real estate as the News Building. Ample windows crowned by a gentle arch gave clear views of the bustling streets.

Marla raised the collar of her jacket and traipsed to her burgundy Toyota 4Runner. Today's wardrobe consisted of a rosy, red blouse over tailored pants. Loose ends of her hair were expertly styled away from her eyes. But if this article was going to shine, she'd better slip into the skin of the down and out—those whose lives had come to a point of desperation.

How an ill-fated decision could lead one down a path they never intended.

As she neared the mission, a neon sign in the window of a restored cottage for honeymooners blinked "No Vacancies."

At the security gate, she flashed her press badge and was waved through where she drove a couple hundred yards along a gravel lot.

The Rose of Sharon compound was arranged in the form of a horseshoe. A wide main building sheathed in metal siding dominated the upper bend. To the right of it sat the historic, log hewn J. Weaver Chapel. Housing units in various stages of stability flanked each side of the property.

A bullying wind resisted Marla's tug on the front door of the main building. The interior smelled of age, old paint, and overcooked casserole. Surely the director had their own private spot where they did whatever was required to successfully manage the organization.

As Marla panned a glance around, her gaze stilled at a placard on the wall.

> If anyone sees a brother or sister in
> need but has no pity on them,
> how can the love of God be in
> them? Mercy triumphs over
> judgment. If not accompanied
> by action, faith is dead.
> I John 3:17, James 2:12, 17

The air went stony silent. Heads turned in Marla's direction and pinned her to the wall.

Kitchen chatter dissipated.

She sounded a nervous cough.

Guests moved through a food line and, taking their plates, sat at various tables.

A mature man serving at the food line broke her stare. "Welcome to the Rose. Please, help yourself to Tuesday's special." He gestured to aluminum pans of stew, pale broccoli, macaroni and cheese, and dinner rolls.

"Oh. No, thanks." She pressed a hand to her middle. "I'm here to meet with—"

He held out a paper plate. His toothy smile conveyed that there was no other place on the planet he would rather be than in a drab, depressing rescue center. "Feel free to take seconds, if you need."

Seconds? Marla doubted she'd be able to stomach the first plate. Why was she, a notable columnist, here again?

The director had to be attending a board meeting or off site, treating potential benefactors to a swanky lunch. She had no idea how these places operated or why anyone would choose to commit time and resources to its cause. But the heart of the one who did begged her consideration—and the attention of her readers.

Out of respect, she accepted the lukewarm food and smiled her thanks.

Clustered at an elongated table near the back wall, several men engaged in jovial conversation as though this were King Henry the VIII's banquet hall. For them, maybe it was.

One could amass material wealth and still be considered a pauper.

She set her plate down and jotted the thought on her iPad.

Mid-day sun streamed through blinds covering the windows that ran along the wall and spotlighted the gathering. She navigated her way past several sullen gazes and approached the men.

"Hello, gentlemen. Marla Mavis here." She added a little wave to an exaggerated smile.

Their faces registered a mix of disinterest and unfamiliarity.

Who didn't know the social columnist of the *Wild Rose Observer*? But then again, those who *did* know her name didn't truly know her. Aside from the benevolent mystery person, no one did—or cared enough to know.

A salty older gentleman stood and proffered a hand. "Name is Oscar Baldwin."

Readily, she accepted his leathery hand. "Hi, Oscar. I work for the Observer. I'm doing a write-up on the Rose of Sharon."

For the love of remarkable news, they had far greater

concerns than her image and couldn't possibly appreciate what was at stake if she botched this assignment.

One austerely handsome client in his, oh, early thirties stood out among the bunch. His pretty-boy features suggested he was younger than what his underlying, rugged maturity conveyed.

The hint of a grin rose on his tanned face. A pleasing auburn scruff shadowed his jaw. Lazy waves of long, dirty blonde hair fell over a set of broad shoulders. He could easily double as a detective on *Hawaii Five-O*—if he'd been stranded on an island, miles from a barber. Any of the pro stylists at Shearly Amazing could do wonders with that hair.

His gently angled brows and liquid gold gaze were marked by lines of compassion and communicated a refreshing selflessness.

He stood and gestured. "Join us?"

She sat, shamelessly running her gaze up his definitively fit stature and firm arms. Her gaze braked at a solid abdomen underneath a long-sleeve, white waffle knit shirt.

When she returned her gaze back to his, he held a stare for several agonizing seconds as though unabashed by the indulgence.

Averting her eyes, she moved the stew around on her plate. Her core turned rubbery.

Gracious, she hadn't come to eat or stare like a lovesick teenager on prom night. She had work to do and a limited amount of time to do it.

Taking her napkin, she dotted the sides of her mouth. "Could anyone tell me where I might find the director?"

A few smirks and shifty gazes flamed up her spine.

Mr. Handsome *and Homeless* nodded. "Follow me."

"Thank you. Where do I take my plate?"

"Leave it on the table. One of the residents will take care of it."

Standing, Marla attempted to meet his gaze but he stood several inches taller than her five feet, six inches.

An infernally long time passed between them. The familiarity—*that presence*—wouldn't let up.

"Mind if I ask your name?"

The client's lazy grin deepened an adorable set of dimples, which she stupidly catalogued in her mind.

"Not at all."

Silence.

"And … it is—?"

She added an exaggerated lilt to her tone to chisel out a response.

At this rate, she'd have the article written by her sixtieth birthday.

A glint of disappointment dimmed his gaze as though his intent to make a guessing game of the social norm of name exchanges lost its fun factor.

"Monroe. Sebastian Monroe," he finally said.

Couldn't be. No!

Marla smacked a palm to her forehead and shook her head.

A steeled expression ran over his hard features.

"Benedict's twin brother?"

For crying over spilled coffee, what horrible fate had befallen Sebastian Monroe after graduation that left him down and out? Granted, he was never the sharpest pencil in the box, especially compared to Benedict.

Marla and Sebastian started their senior year as casual friends and members of the high school service club, but

Marla feared she'd tarnish her popular girl reputation if she got chummy with an unmotivated type who'd been seen sleeping at his desk.

He wound that set of well-developed arms into a knot. The sleeve of his shirt strained against a prominent bicep. "Yeah. Benny's twin."

"Surprised to see you back in the Ridge, Seb."

A shadow rumbled over his forehead. "No one calls me that."

"I used to." Her arms fell lax at her sides. "Before you distanced yourself from me."

Even if reasons were fuzzy, a keen girl knew when a guy had raised a drawbridge on her account.

"Hard to trust someone who's got no respect for you."

"You're still bitter about that?"

"You voted me least likely to succeed, Marla."

"It wasn't meant to be taken seriously."

"Anything that's printed for all eyes to read should be taken seriously."

She didn't come here to spar with past history, but the providential exchange with Sebastian might deliver brilliant gems of information. But how would it reflect on the town if she spun the story that one of the Ridge's own hadn't fared well and today, relied on said town for food and shelter?

It would be premature to coax backstory that led to Sebastian's predicament, but something didn't quite fit the picture. And she was determined to put the pieces together.

The weight of responsibility increased.

She fired up her notes app on her iPad. "How long have you been with the program?"

"A month."

Her heels clicked over the tile as she strode in Sebastian's shadow to a hallway off the kitchen. He withdrew an impressive collection of keys and unlocked a door marked 'Director'.

"Good behavior must lend itself to being entrusted with a set of keys," she said in a nervous laugh-giggle.

Inside the door, he flipped a switch. Overhead light illuminated the modest space filled with mis-matched shelving units. Canned goods and paper products sagged the shelves. An opposite wall held floor-to-ceiling boxes.

Two blinks later, she grimaced at him. "No desk or chairs? No file cabinets, decorative lamps, or even a pretty plant?"

"Donations have been pouring in after a recent campaign sponsored by Rosehill Church. We needed the space."

A guffaw. "What director is crazy enough to give up their office?"

"I am."

Her lungs clenched, strained the flow of air. "You're, you're—?"

"The director."

Chapter Two

Just great. Sebastian Monroe's humble world of service as a humanitarian had collided with Marla's, his future now in the hands of a gossip columnist. Good thing he was only sojourning through the Ridge, the place where she'd decimated his ego—using the power of printed media to do it.

Nothing would convince him she wouldn't go to great lengths to write something humiliating again. This time, she wielded a note-taking app and the ability to smear his good name, along with the organization he was fiercely determined to revive.

As to that endeavor, he hadn't made enough progress. What if he failed in the midst of her snooping around in his business? What if her snooping contributed to his failure?

Sheesh.

Yes, the Rose of Sharon needed solid exposure if he had any hope of breathing new life into it. But why did it have to come by way of … her?

Worse, he hated himself for being unable to stop caring about Marla Mavis. She still had that infuriating ability to make him want to lower to one knee and promise his undying love.

By month's end, he hoped to begin a new job with Samaritan's Purse, Berlin, Germany. At long last, a stable source of income, doing what he loved.

The force of Marla's essence slammed through his body long before it smacked his senses. To the residents of Wild Rose Ridge, she was the gossip columnist. To him, she was the organically beautiful girl he couldn't shake. But his low-profile profession pitted against her highly touted persona meant they'd have no reason to cross paths.

No cause for concern.

Then why hadn't Sebastian's heart stopped thumping from the time she entered the building?

Marla's shameless gaze settled around his shoulders, flitted down to his boots, and back up. "Looks like you've invested a good bit of time at the gym since graduation."

"The nature of humanitarian relief work requires me to stay in shape."

"Still as loyal to a cause as I remember." She squinted at him. "Are you sure you're not the new and improved version of your twin brother?"

He raised a two-finger salute. "Scout's honor. Voted most unlikely to succeed."

Her chin dropped to her chest. "Guess that wasn't my greatest moment," she muttered.

In his estimation, it was the worst.

"You wrote what you believed." And, according to Benedict, commandeered the yearbook committee to print the senior class voting results in the yearbook, publish the outcome in the school newspaper, and blast it on the PA.

Shards of memory stabbed at his heart.

"Are you done here?"

"A quick perusal of your make-shift storage unit is hardly sufficient data. I'll need more from you."

Now, if that didn't strike fear. Marla was a dog with a bone. Pity the guy who'd been bitten by her.

Emotions threatened to short circuit his brain. *Shake it off, man!*

In addition to delivering an addictive dose of lethal femininity, she came packaged in temptation that could easily sever common sense from his brain like a meat cleaver.

A call from Pastor Michael Chandler of Rosehill Community Church chimed on his phone. He raised a finger at Marla and answered. "Sebastian Monroe." He drew his voice away and nodded in succession to communicate supreme preoccupation.

"Yep, sure thing. I can take care of that." He grabbed a napkin, scrawled on it. "Fifty you said?" More nodding. "We'll have them ready for distribution this Saturday at 11. Thanks."

When Sebastian ended the call, he found Marla trekking a wary glance around the interior. Out of her comfort zone, it seemed. But then again, their zones never did align.

"Gotta run, Marla. Busy week."

"When would be a good time for me to sit down with you and ask questions?"

"I rarely sit."

"I'm a reporter. I need answers. Can't you spare a few minutes to help a girl out?"

Ah, his kryptonite.

Of all the women in all the universe who needed his help, he'd been placed in the same galaxy with this one.

Why, Lord?

The longer he spent time with her, the greater risk there'd be little to nothing left of him—his stubborn heart cast to the vultures of wishful thinking. But far be it for Sebastian to neglect someone's need when it was in his power to ease the burden.

But the Ridge's lauded and loved media girl would have to work for it.

"Saturday morning. Be here by 5:00."

Her eyes went wild. "Why so early?"

"We need time to prepare breakfast. It's served at 7."

She gaped at him as though he'd skinned her cat. No doubt she still owned at least one clawing, prowling feline.

"I can't get solid answers while you're scrambling eggs … or whatever you'll be doing."

He leaned a shoulder on the wall and crossed his ankles. "Coffee is on me."

She gave an indignant sputter. "I cannot be coerced by way of coffee."

"Dark roast with a hint of cinnamon and a dollop of whipped cream. Two sugars." Just the way she liked it.

He hung his apron on a hook before turning to see her mouth opened partly, her brow drawn tight.

"For all you know, I despise coffee."

"In high school, you deemed it a food group. It would take some doing to convince me that's changed."

A smile of fascination tipped the edges of Marla's glossy lips. "You remember."

Wished he could forget.

According to Sebastian's inside source at the hospital, Marla had rallied from cancer treatments and surgery. Today she was the picture of health and vitality. Aside from having recovered a full head of hair—the slick sheen of red-orange playing in the light—and a refreshingly soft demeanor, not much had changed about Marla.

He followed her to her car, doing his level best to ignore the dizzying effect of her perfectly shaped curves.

Unexpectedly, she turned and fixed a studied curiosity on him.

A shiver ran over his shoulders.

He swallowed against the impact of her nearness. The thump of longing against his ribs rivaled a marching band.

"See you Saturday," she said, taking slow, backward steps.

"Bright and early," he called back in provocation.

"Early, Seb. That's all I promise."

Insufferable man!

Marla was unaccustomed to being challenged by someone who had the upper hand. She could think of a million alternatives to her hard-earned Saturday morning than playing sous-chef to Sebastian. How cleverly he'd whisked her into his territory to do his bidding.

"Two can play at this game. I'll just wait around until

breakfast has been served, then pin him down for the answers I need."

Clanks and clinks and the spit of frying bacon drew her through the dining area where Sebastian met her in the open door.

"You're late," he said, handing her a capped cup of hot coffee.

"By fifteen minutes," she said, taking a sip of the steamy brew, blended to perfection.

"Then you're fifteen minutes late."

She twirled the end of her hair. "Which would matter if I were the bride and you were the groom."

A delicious crackle of tension popped before Sebastian's brows cinched.

Low chatter drifted from around a partitioned wall. Oscar and a shaggy-haired man in his 30s donned aprons and busied themselves cracking eggs and retrieving items from a walk-in refrigerator. The kitchen's homey scent stoked memories of Mom which stoked memories Marla really couldn't afford to nurture right now.

Threads of loneliness went taut. Would she die alone too? Her own father—whoever he was—didn't stick around after Mom told him she was pregnant with her.

At the ring of a landline, Sebastian disappeared into an adjoining hallway and answered. "Hello, this is Sebastian, Director."

Hmm. Not just anyone had skill enough to manage an organization of this complexity. She knew enough that the Rose of Sharon served a broad area which meant Sebastian's position required supreme flexibility, preparedness, and discernment.

Establishing trust among Sebastian's subordinates and

clients was paramount. He showed no signs of arrogance or dominance over the people under his authority. He treated everyone as an equal. Like family.

He'd once confessed that his family life hadn't been a happy one. She never bothered to ask why.

Exhaustion gnawed at her bones. She brought her hand to her mouth to stifle a yawn tickling her throat.

"Don't that beat all."

Marla left Sebastian to his conversation and turned to see Oscar scratching at his gray temple. He gave his saggy jeans an upward tug and turned to the other man who commanded the stove. "We're short on milk for the scrambled eggs."

Marla wandered over. "When I cooked with my mom, she would sometimes substitute water for milk. Then she'd add a dash or two more salt. Couldn't tell the difference."

"Mornin', Miss Mavis," Oscar said. "This is Leonard Crenshaw. Recent graduate of the year-long residential program. Mr. Bash hired him to work for the Rose."

Marla smiled a greeting at the man who went by Leonard. "Pleased to meet you."

"We're grateful you chose to help us out." Oscar handed Marla a whisk. "Care to give the eggs a stir?"

Marla shrank back.

Oscar laughed. His yellowed, misaligned teeth flashed below a bushy mustache. "It won't bite."

"But I might."

That huffed response from a stout woman of hearty German stock who barreled in. She wore a hairnet over a tightly coiled silvery-blonde bun and paired a navy pullover with stretch knit, dark pants.

The woman thrust a plump hand to her hip and ran a

disconcerting gaze up and down Marla's frame. "I'm Hilda. Kitchen manager. You must be the newspaper woman Bash was telling us about."

Sebastian had spoken of her? "Yes. Ma'am."

Hilda used her forefinger and thumb to massage her chin. "One of the many things I admire about Bash is his ability to see good in someone that others can't. Now then, those eggs won't scramble themselves." Hilda handed her an apron. "You'll want to protect that pretty raspberry colored shirt."

Mercy, how had the tables turned since she stepped into this place?

Abandoning her brew, Marla slowly fastened the apron and took the whisk from Oscar whose gaze indicated amusement. She stirred the eggs to a golden yellow.

Heated ovens delivered the sugary scents of a bakery.

Oscar pulled out an odd assortment of puff pastries, cinnamon rolls, and donuts. He placed the tray at the end of the counter, then set out chilled juice boxes and water bottles. Two urns of coffee percolated along a far wall.

"When our guests come through the line, we serve them a generous portion of eggs, two strips of bacon or sausage links, a pastry, and fruit cup," Hilda said.

Marla hadn't asked for a tutorial. Certainly hadn't signed up to scoop eggs. But her conscience would not allow her to refuse to assist this skeleton crew.

From yards away, the Bible verse screamed off the wall. *If anyone sees a brother or sister in need but has no pity on them ...*

Ending his call, Sebastian breezed over to a side door to welcome a lineup of haggard people, shivering in the stinging air.

"Good morning, my friends," Sebastian said. "Come inside where it's warm. Breakfast is about ready."

Making their way through the line, several guests raised a hand to Sebastian who addressed them by name and clapped a high-five in the manner of a proud coach after a winning game.

My, how he worked his magic to bring smiles to these gaunt faces.

Sebastian motioned for Marla to stand beside him where he served a heap of eggs, bacon, or sausage to guests as they moved along.

Taking tongs, Marla served pastries.

Leonard and Oscar added sides and a beverage.

A meager cost-per-plate, prepared from donated and wholesale foodstuffs, yet the offering was received as though they'd labored for days to prepare a feast fit for the Queen of England.

The experience was oddly satisfying. Elation unspooled and traveled into her pores. Everyone needed to experience this!

When viewed through the grander scheme of weighty issues, was Marla doing all she could with what God had given her? Why couldn't the content of Marla's Musings go beyond reporting smitten couples in town to inspiring others to give and serve generously?

The Rose of Sharon had been established in the Ridge three decades ago. It required constant support from the community but had faltered under the last director's care.

Why hadn't Sebastian utilized the full power of the press?

Once the equipment had been cleaned and put to rights and the dining area ordered and sanitized, Oscar, Leonard, and a few other able-bodied helpers transitioned to outside tasks while Hilda reviewed inventory, murmuring in German.

For a moment, Marla lost sight of Sebastian. A disquieting sensation of being unmoored and adrift overtook her.

When he reappeared, wearing a smile, the sensation evaporated.

"Hope this experience has given you useful content."

"It's a start."

He was quick to pull a pamphlet. "Here's a summary of the mission. It's a little dated, but you might find something of interest in it."

"It's not the mission I have questions about. It's you."

A dark disturbance dimmed Sebastian's gaze. He yanked off his apron, rotated a metal chair, and sat hard.

"I won't get very far if you're uncooperative."

"The Rose requires the strength of many. This isn't about me."

Hilda tromped through the dining area with a clipboard. "I'm headed to Gus's Groceries. Need you to review and approve the order."

Sebastian gave the order a quick perusal, then jotted his signature at the bottom.

Marla took a mental screenshot of his unique penmanship. The long, narrowed stretch of the script and severe angle suggested he was a confident man with a large heart and lofty goals, but the illegibility might mean a need to conceal his identity and keep himself small.

But why?

Sebastian returned the order and pen to Hilda. "When you're there, please remember to ask how Gus's dog Piper is doing. He had to take her to Dr. Beringer at the vet hospital."

"We'd make our dollars stretch a lot further if we purchased from a national grocery chain."

Sebastian gave Hilda a little pat on the shoulder. "But that doesn't benefit Gus, now does it."

"As you wish, Bash."

Even Broom Hilda had come under his spell.

At Hilda's exit, Sebastian rested his arms over the back of the chair.

At long last, his undivided attention.

"All right, Sebastian, I've given my time freely today. Now, we follow my agenda."

His teasing grins were beginning to erode her sense of composure. Her heart could not afford to enjoy one skinny second of this.

She unfastened her apron and sat opposite him—if for no other reason than to distance herself from the electricity sparking in her middle when he gazed at her as though admiring art.

She was no Mona Lisa!

Marla drew out her iPad pencil. "Tell me why you took this job?"

"There was a need."

"Do you always jump at an opportunity when there's a need?"

"I agreed to answer questions about the ministry."

"The way I see it, you're its source of oxygen. The two are inexorably connected, which means, for the time being, you and I are inexorably connected."

He came to his feet and took long strides toward the kitchen.

She scurried after him, bumping against the solid musculature of his back when he halted near a stainless steel counter.

Oof! She spit out a cough.

"Sorry," he said, a bit wild-eyed but with a hint of mirth.

"Do you ever stay in one spot for more than five minutes?" she sputtered.

"We open the dining hall again at 11." He gestured to a wall clock. "But the lunch crowd lines up as early as 10:30."

Leonard appeared, balancing a large tray that held deli meat and cheese slices. "Where to, Bash?"

Sebastian tapped the counter. "Here is fine for now."

Leonard faltered. The tray wobbled.

Marla steadied it on one side.

"Appreciate that, Ma'am."

"Glad I could help," she said.

Grinning, Sebastian stepped around Marla. He leaned remarkably close as he reached for something on a shelf behind her. The masculine scent of cedar wood and strength razzed her senses.

Pulling back, he uncapped a water bottle and guzzled it, then locked an indecipherable gaze on her.

A moment of sexual tension purred between them. She blinked free from the slow burn of desire, though the heat of his essence surrounding her was quickly becoming inescapable.

To let herself fall for him ... for any man again ... promised an unhappy ending.

"We'll create an assembly line to prepare and bag

sandwiches, add chips, a protein bar, a pudding cup, and water bottles into fifty paper bags."

"I need my questions answered."

Sebastian crushed the water bottle in his palm like it was a paper receipt and tossed it in a recycling bin. "I need volunteer spirit."

She sneered at him which only intensified the attractiveness of his stalwart aura.

He wiggled the box of disposable gloves at her. "Ready to line up?"

Chapter Three

If the business of doing good deeds was contagious, Marla had been deliciously infected by it. Given last Saturday's benevolent companion, she was not altogether upset by the condition either.

"Earth to Marla."

Sparing Marla a reckless reverie, Lorraine gave her hands a clap. "Is the fact that you're on Fiona's podcast at the bookstore this afternoon behind the preoccupied expression?"

Was is Tuesday already?

Marla shook her head.

"Then it must be your ex's second attempt to repair the damage he's done."

Hardly. "Tickets to the Bradshaw family rodeo next month is tempting, but no."

Lorraine narrowed her gaze. "Then what's distracting you?"

Past history, missed moments. Deep regret.

If Sebastian was the right man, Marla would be the greatest disappointment.

He deserved a saint!

Marla gripped her jacket lapels and cinched them over the front her cherry red top. If someone had told her that she'd one day become smitten by Sebastian Monroe, yesterday's lanky, unimpressive guy, she'd have scoffed. But few things were more attractive than a man of integrity who disdained hero status.

Her interest in what drove Sebastian to sacrifice his ambitions for the good of others dominated her thoughts.

Who took care of Sebastian? What were his goals for the future? Did they include a wife and kids?

Behind her pursuit of highlighting the merits of a struggling small-town ministry simmered a bubbling interest in … him.

"In order to regain Sebastian Monroe's trust, I have to maintain a bird's eye view in my reporting and give him no street credit."

"Sebastian?"

"The director of the Rose of Sharon."

"Ah, promising. First name basis already."

"Because I knew him in high school."

Lorraine pulled a chair and sat like she was poised to watch a film. "You two have a history?"

"Yes and no."

In the spirit of Scotland Yard, Lorraine leaned forward and pressed her palms on top of the desk. "That statement violates the Law of Noncontradiction. Either you did or you did not."

"His family moved to the Ridge at the start of our

freshman year, but we didn't hang out much. There was this one memorable night though."

A Cheshire cat smile tipped the edges of Lorraine's lips. "Do tell."

"It wasn't like that." The reel played in Marla's head again. Taking her mug of coffee, Marla wandered to the window and sipped the tepid brew.

Street traffic hummed below. The sky was clear, the glass cold to touch.

"Sebastian and I were in the same service club. Our group learned about a single mother who lost her job and needed a twin bed for her daughter. The situation was not unlike my mom's struggle. My friend and I drove to the woman's apartment to deliver a bed anonymously, but Sebastian was already there doing the same, only he added a comforter, pillow, and bedsheets. Plus huge boxes of snacks and cases of water."

"Did Sebastian see you?"

"We spoke briefly, but I'd stupidly mistook him for his brother Benedict and wrote about his generous deed in the school paper." She returned to her desk. "It was Benedict who corrected me."

Silent as a lamb to slaughter, Sebastian allowed the accolade to fall to the wrong person. Maybe he'd lost trust that she would ever write anything nice about him.

"That night, God showcased Sebastian's passionate heart, but I was too self-absorbed to appreciate it. When I found out at summer camp that Mom lost her battle with cancer, his was the only show of sympathy I received."

"Touching."

"It was everything. His awkward side hug amounted to an embrace by a prince."

"Mmm. If you write this well, you'd not only redeem yourself in his eyes, but you'll do him and the Rose of Sharon a great service."

"I can't." Marla released a labored sigh. "He refuses to have his name associated with the piece."

"You must. People will be so fired up, he'll have to turn down applicants and volunteers."

What was supposed to be a broad-sweeping general news story was transitioning to a human-interest piece—Marla's interest in said human breaking through her emotional boundary lines.

But there were holes in her article, the research spotty and vague. This would never satisfy Cecilia or the public or contest judges, for that matter. She'd be a joke among the industry.

Unscripted, authentic moments were the stuff media and the public voraciously consumed. But for Marla to capture Sebastian in the wild, it would require dogged determination to carve out time to volunteer—no more than an hour at a time, mind you—without involving a sliver more of her heart.

Since Sebastian's return to the Ridge, he committed to stop into Rosehips, a bookshop on Main Street, to greet Benedict who worked the register.

Benedict was a fastidious intellect who thrived on fact-finding and had out-smarted national exams. His academic prowess had earned him a degree in linguistics and archival history. He'd worked various jobs at the universities and as a museum curator which ultimately led him to this sleepy bookstore in Wild Rose Ridge.

Earlier that morning, a text notification alerted Sebastian that the books he'd ordered for the new reading and literacy program had arrived.

But today's visit would have to be brief. He couldn't afford another encounter with those three meddling women —Diana Alexander, Barbara Schulte and her sister Lorraine—who'd dominated his front stoop last evening with their cat-ate-the-mouse smiles.

Under the guise of a late welcome, the three musketeers delivered a hot meal that came booby trapped with a litany of brow-wiggling questions.

Apparently, the wires of hot topics were abuzz in their knitting circle about Marla's time at the Rose of Sharon last Saturday. Her zest for championing his cause to revive the place must have ignited their agenda to make an item out of him and Marla.

A bell over the door chimed through the bookstore. The aromatic scent of tea and musty books permeated the air. People sat in quiet reading corners at the front window and near a tea prep area in the back. High and low bookshelves held a variety of old volumes.

When Sebastian approached the counter, Benedict's nose remained in the spine of a book.

Unlike Sebastian, an impressive IQ had been woven into Benedict's DNA, but also unlike Sebastian, the poor guy had the social skills and engaging personality of a cactus.

Sebastian gave Benedict's pencil thin arm a soft jab. "How's it going today, Benny?"

Slowly, Benedict lowered a hardbound copy of

Dostoyevsky's *Crime and Punishment.* Imaginary stars swirled over his head as though he'd traveled in a time machine back to the present. A scowl communicated he was none too pleased about it.

Sebastian drummed his fingers. "I could have been an armed thief or the mayor on official business."

"You, the mayor?"

Leaving the insult alone, Sebastian rested a lazy arm on the counter. "Sell a lot of books today?"

Benedict narrowed his gaze as though deciphering Morse code.

Sebastian gave the dumb book a hard flick with his finger. "These things, Benny. Sell many?"

"Plenty enough." Benedict closed the book and set it gingerly to the side as though it were on loan from the Library of Congress.

"I've come to pick up the books we ordered for the Rose of Sharon."

From behind him, Benedict retrieved a box that caused him to bobble.

Sebastian skirted the counter and eased the load onto a level surface.

"What's the status of the mission?" Benedict said, returning to his post at the register.

"Busy. The previous director left me with a two-person staff to manage the kitchen, programs, housing, and grounds keeping. Before the next director takes over, I intend to build that up, put more muscle into reaching more of our homeless population, and develop a stronger volunteer base."

"Why can't that director be you?"

"I don't live here."

"You're perfectly suited to fill the position."

"That would require a commitment I'm not able to make."

Benedict pushed his glasses up the bridge of his thin nose. "You're not able to or you won't?"

Aggravation bristled down Sebastian's spine. He cut Benedict a hard glance. "Why the inquisition?"

"I presumed you might find merit in establishing residency for a change."

Despite Sebastian's less-than-successful reputation, he'd taken a crack at earning a degree. But when he heard the news about a catastrophic earthquake in Indonesia, he couldn't justify listening to a droning professor expound on the periodic table. Knowing the order of the elements never put food in the bellies of starving villagers.

One mission led to another, enabling Sebastian to travel from place to place, keeping his heart a veritable moving target. Because if the girl he secretly adored in high school could deem him unsuccessful, any woman could.

"In my quest to serve in all seven continents, I still lack Australia and Antarctica," Sebastian finally said.

The click of heels from the back of the store offered reprieve from Benedict's reticent gaze. Sebastian turned to see Marla Mavis striding his direction with intention and purpose.

A form-fitting knit dress nicely hugged her curves … if he were looking.

When Marla came within a few feet, her intoxicating fragrance of flowers and dauntlessness held him spellbound. A wicked aphrodisiac.

Would he ever forget this woman? She'd decimated his

character. Why allow her any real estate in his heart? Surely there was a good man in this town who would love her well and commit himself to her welfare.

"If I remember from high school, you weren't always punctual," Marla said.

"Said the girl who arrived late last Saturday."

"If we were getting married, I would have been on time."

She gave him a playful shoulder shove.

His pulse thundered in his ears. He widened his stance to regain balance. Was she making a mockery of the idea of marrying him? If it weren't for the fragile threads of hope he detected in her whimsical gaze, he'd bet on it.

"But I'm relieved to see you made this a priority. Fiona is ready for us," she said.

"To do what?"

She returned a 'don't be silly' grin and tugged his arm.

He stutter-stepped behind her into a media studio where Fiona rose from a swivel chair and shook his hand.

"Good to see you, Sebastian." Fiona gave her head a slow shake and chuckled. "I must admit, I struggle to believe you and Benedict are brothers."

Their life pursuits looked nothing alike either.

Sure, Sebastian had struggled academically, but he could mobilize warring parties to sign a peace treaty with a smile and a handshake.

While those assets hadn't been enough to impress Marla, they served Sebastian well in his endeavors. Suffering communities didn't care about a guy's resume. They only needed the hands and feet of Jesus—in which case, Sebastian excelled.

But now his humanitarian success had come under Marla's scrutiny.

Summoning a measure of defense, Sebastian shut his eyes and read the caption again …

Finally—and to no one's surprise—the most unlikely to succeed is Sebastian Monroe.

Byline? Yeah. Marla Mavis.

Marla, the only woman he'd ever considered marrying. The beautiful school girl with friends a plenty but who were absent her during her darkest days.

Marla's beautiful face came into Sebastian's field of focus. He blinked out of a prolonged stare, cleared his throat, and addressed Fiona. "Appearances can be—" He slid Marla a glance. "Deceiving."

Widening his perusal of the studio, he took in the formality of the space marked by a desk, sound equipment, and recording devices.

Marla squeezed his hand rather possessively. "Don't be nervous. Let's just take the interview where it will."

"Interview!?" he balked within a tinny laugh.

Fiona snapped a mic on his collar like it was a carabiner clip.

He drew in a hard breath. "There must be some mistake. I'm here to pick up books."

Fiona and Marla leaned away from one another and exchanged perplexed glances.

Sebastian noted the bob in Marla's throat. "You forwarded the email invite to him, right?"

"I think so." Fiona said, nodding. Then a head shake, a shrug. "I've been so distracted preparing for new book arrivals and wrapping up winter inventory. But no worries.

The paperwork isn't a prerequisite for being a guest on the show."

Wait … show?!

Fiona shifted on the stool and gestured for Sebastian and Marla to sit opposite the kidney bean shaped-desk.

The gentle force of Marla's touch on his shoulder caused his legs to bend at her will.

The walls closed in.

He sprang to his feet.

The protrusive mic near his mouth swung upward.

He reached to straighten the stand, then swiped his clammy hands down the sides of his pants.

Stepping backward, an awkward laugh slipped out. "If you'll excuse me, ladies, I really can't spare the time."

Marla patted the seat. "I've seen your skeleton crew. I know the impact this will have when people are quickened to the need. Let the media help you."

Heat flamed up his neck. He glowered at her. But in all fairness, the irresponsibility of the media at the Monroe family's expense when he and Benedict were impressionable kids wasn't Marla's fault. The article she'd published in the high school yearbook—complete with a photo of him dozing at his desk in social studies? *That* was entirely her doing.

Not again. Sebastian was no friend of the media.

His voice rose to barely above a whisper, strained by emotion. "God will provide."

God, please provide a director to replace me!

Chapter Four

Outside the bookstore, Marla managed to intercept Sebastian's evasion with a grip on his upper arm. The counter-pressure of his flexed bicep was an exhilarating fringe benefit to an otherwise routine podcast.

"You and I are today's guest on the show. You can't leave me to do this interview alone."

He bowed his chest. "I have clients that need me."

She stood heel-to-boot with him. "That's the whole point. Your clients and their need."

The notch between his brow deepened.

"Look, I'm sorry this caught you off guard, but I'm only trying to help your cause."

He set his arms low at his hips and leaned on one leg as though postured to launch into a sprint.

"That broody expression tells me you're unhappy."

He didn't flinch.

She dared a wink. Got nothing.

"Aw, c'mon, Seb. I've watched how congenial you are

with people. So refreshingly blind to status, racial, or religious differences that I mistook you for a homeless man."

"People are people. No one is above need."

"See what I mean? You possess an admirable, infectious, and rare perspective."

To each point, she poked a finger at his chest and found it as sturdy as it looked.

The side of his mouth drew slightly into a sidelong grin. Images of those husky, long-haired models on the cover of romance novels passed like moving pictures in her head.

Suddenly, she relished her job.

"In my research, I found the information on the Rose of Sharon outdated and unimpressive. I intend for this article to light a fire in people, far and wide."

"Since my boots hit the ground, I've seen plenty of fire in the people around town for good causes."

"Yes, if they're informed. The only event that doesn't require excessive PR is the men's shirtless volleyball tournament at Beach Park in December. No one misses that fundraiser, and, believe me, you'll be a tough contender this year."

"I won't be here beyond March."

Sadness clogged her throat. She swallowed past it. "You already found a replacement?"

He gave his head an infinitesimal shake and scraped his fingers through that luscious head of sun-kissed hair.

"This makes no sense. You need PR which I have in spades, and I need your cooperation to write a winning article."

"I don't want to be put on the spot."

"Yet you won't hesitate to jet to the far side of the

planet for a good cause but come unglued in a little tourist town when the need is equally worthy."

"Because minutes can make the difference between life and death. I saw unspeakable conditions during the last several years. There really are no adequate words to convey the depth of need."

If she got him talking, she'd have remarkable content. A top news story the town wouldn't stop talking about. She'd break free from the realm of ordinary and superficial.

The readers of Wild Rose Ridge would soon meet the new Marla Mavis!

Taking two steps closer, she entered the dangerous realm of his masculinity. "May I quote you?"

"No."

She frowned. "I get this sense that you believe it's your responsibility to fix all that's broken in the world. To get an 'atta boy' from God or even outperform him."

Storm clouds rumbled in his darkened gaze. "You're putting words in my mouth," he groused.

She'd studied his behavior enough to know it was to her benefit to clip the conversation there. If she pushed boundaries, her article would read like the Internal Revenue Manual for filing taxes.

"Can I still count on you at the mission tomorrow?" he said, his tone tenuous.

"I've blocked off an hour each day, Monday through Friday."

"I'll take it. We hold a small group Bible study every Wednesday at 2 in the Weaver Chapel."

Only one of the most romantic historical locations in town!

According to city records, Judah Weaver, the great grandfather of Reuben Weaver—proprietor of Hanford's Jewelers on Main Street—built that rustic wood chapel in anticipation of marrying his mail-order bride, Priscilla.

Against the odds, their marriage lasted till death parted them. Any marriage founded on a commitment to love and serve one another ought to endure.

Short-circuiting her fantasy, Sebastian added, "I welcome everyone and pray a blessing. Then Pastor Michael Chandler and his wife Leilah lead the group."

Marla could use a blessing about now. Particularly one offered in a rustic, sacred setting by a man who looked very much like he spent time among the angels and emanated the warmth of God's light.

Oh, she was losing her grip. She must end this or she'd faint and embarrass herself.

"The members would be encouraged to see a show of community support," he prompted.

"You promise no egg scrambling?"

At her return to an innocuous subject, his posture eased.

A low laugh accompanied his advance. He narrowed the distance perilously close and glanced down at her. "No eggs will be scrambled."

"All right, then. I'll see you tomorrow."

Tomorrow was a thousand years.

He nodded and turned to leave, then pivoted in a half turn. "One more thing." A shy grin drew at his mouth. "Don't come as Marla Mavis, a news writer. Just come as you are."

"Who would that be, Seb?"

Glittery pixie dust puffed over his head. He kicked at a stone that pinged off the curb.

"A survivor."

The following afternoon, Sebastian entered the J. Weaver Chapel. Large scale windows on one side provided the worshiper a view of its grander counterpart, Rosehill Community Church—the crown jewel of the southwest ridgeline.

Support groups met in what was originally designed as a pastoral side room for private study.

Sebastian arranged logs within a stone-cut hearth and built a toasty fire. A sofa and chairs furnished the space that soon grew to a comfortable warmth.

A coffee table held pastries provided by Weaver's Bakery and coffee from Magic Beans Coffee Shop.

Sebastian's cell rang. At long last, he had an HR representative of Samaritan's Purse on the line. The conversation flowed effortlessly until …

"We need you to give us an affirmative date on your availability in order to hold the spot. Otherwise—"

"No, sir," Sebastian said. "I'm definitely interested. It's just that I don't have a viable candidate to fill the position. Yet."

The weighty pause hammered in Sebastian's chest.

Pastor Michael's and Leilah's playful banter drifted over as they entered the room.

Sebastian acknowledged the flirty power team with a

smile and nod, then hung back in the chapel beneath a vaulted ceiling.

"Sure hope that deal shakes out soon. Based on what we know of your work ethic and heart for people, you'd be our top choice. Pays well, benefits go without saying. You'd have lodging and transportation covered."

A dream job with a reputable organization that checked all the boxes. It would enable Sebastian to continue the pace of lateral mobility. An added bonus, he'd keep his heart a moving target.

"Count on me. I'll be available by month's end."

But if he couldn't keep a small-town ministry to the homeless population from going under, how could he ever fulfill the expectations of a world-wide ministry?

God was big enough to take care of people outside Sebastian's reach. Had Marla detected misplaced motivation behind his drive and determination?

Would she take her probing suspicions to the press and smear his name?

A D+ student had no business tangling with publicity types. If he let his attraction to Marla linger, she could maul his ego again, this time with the unrelenting ferocity of an Alaskan grizzly.

More than ever, Sebastian needed this opportunity. A way out of his obligation in the Ridge before he put his heart on the line for the one woman he could never trust—but would always love.

Such cruel irony.

If Marla kept her promise to show up today, Sebastian determined he'd make a close study of her. Anyone who'd outsmarted death the way she had ought to credit the success to divine intervention.

What role did God play in Marla's life, if any? Had she let hardship strengthen her faith? If she had no interest in things of God, well, that could be a deal breaker.

When Sebastian returned to the room, Pastor Michael and Leilah engaged him in the usual crush of hugs and handshakes.

Michael's cool bravado mixed with the heart of a shepherd had earned him the reputation of the people's pastor. Rosehill's dwindling membership had soared after he was hired.

Leilah kept her stark blond hair choppy. According to Michael, she shared his penchant for tattoos which were largely hidden beneath her black leather jacket.

Despite appearances to the contrary, she'd softened her presentation since she and Michael married, evidenced in her custom jewelry collection sold online as Skye Jewelry.

Years ago, they met in Vegas and fell hard and fast in love—until Michael up and abandoned her. Christmas before last, their lives intersected and God worked a miracle.

Sebastian took a seat in an armchair near Leilah who sat beside Michael on the sofa.

Leilah munched on a frosted sugar cookie, then addressed Sebastian. "Oscar said the patrons are finishing lunch in the dining hall and should be here shortly."

"The men and women coming today responded to my invitation during one of our mobile van outreach efforts."

"Strong work, friend." Michael draped a lazy arm around Leilah and drew her to his side. "A soul who's welcomed with grace and treated with dignity can change the world."

Thing was, not everyone who'd been shot down in life

possessed the resilience to rise above it. Marla had overcome the odds, looking exceptionally well on the other side of them.

Marla, Marla, Marla.

Michael came to the edge of the sofa. "Hey, fearless leader, why don't you pray us off to a good start before they arrive."

"Sure thing." Sebastian postured for prayer. "God, you are a good father. A healer—" He sat ramrod straight. "Wait. Where's Marla?"

Was she still coming? Or was she coddling him?

The door banged open.

Marla, in all her unapologetically feminine glory, scuttled over in a pair of dress boots that met the hem of a fitted skirt. Her long-sleeved blouse with ruffly cuffs was the shade of merlot—shimmery, aromatic, and aged to perfection.

"Sorry, I'm late. I ran into Genevieve Beringer and her husband Adam. Naturally, I had to ask how things were going since they got married."

Her voice withered and shoulders slumped. Momentarily, the fuel drained out of her rocket.

Leilah took another bite of the cookie. "My mom tells me you're a key player in their matchmaking shenanigans."

Taking the chair opposite Sebastian, Marla marvelously recovered her composure. "They call it a knitting circle."

"Everyone knows those ladies use the yarn shop as an outpost for matchmaking council meetings."

"Hey, babe," Michael said to Leilah. "Their meddling worked in our favor."

Leilah returned a foxy smile and boldly kissed Michael on the lips.

Sebastian noted the way Marla's gaze held fast to Michael and Leilah, neither of them coming up for oxygen.

The sheen in Marla's gemstone eyes lost a touch of brilliance as though the encounter had poked at a need.

Maybe a career focused on documenting perfect pairings for a girl who—for reasons Sebastian couldn't figure—hadn't found her own was beginning to lose its appeal.

A thirsty soul using her keen eye for romance and media persuasion to fill other people's wells, draining her sense of worth in the process.

Was Marla's article a strategic move to take her career in a different direction? Did God expect Sebastian to cooperate and give Marla a leg up?

Maybe. But if the Ridge's local gossip columnist intended to achieve her own brand of success, it really *really* should not involve him.

Chapter Five

At the end of the study, the members thanked Pastor Michael, Leilah, Sebastian, and Marla.

Soon, the chapel emptied of everyone but Marla who hadn't removed her gaze from Sebastian. He felt her eyeballs on him like he was a specimen on a glass slide. Assessing, sizing him up. Measuring his validity.

Had he said something stupid? Fallen short in her eyes at some point during the hour?

He shoved his hands in the pockets of his coat and fidgeted with his keys. "Glad you could join us today. This is the heart of what we do here."

"Their stories are touching. Poignant and relatable."

"Your willingness to share what you've been through was invaluable."

Her smile was weak.

"Hopefully you heard something you can use," he said.

Enough to wrap up their temporary arrangement and part ways before the swell of desire for her engulfed him.

"Yes, but what I find utterly fascinating is that you

treat the mundane task of handing a homeless person a sack lunch with as much decency as you do these people's hardships."

Any longer in her presence and he'd lick the plate of respect she'd served clean and forget how to spell his own name.

A pendulum clock near the hearth chimed a quarter past the hour. "Guess it's past time for you to head back to work."

"This is my work. It's the part I love the most. Getting up close and personal."

Showing no signs of urgency to return to the *Observer*, she came to the fireplace and flipped her palms toward the glowing embers. "I've got endless questions."

"Ask away," he said, far too eagerly.

She spun and strode over to him. "Why aren't you married?"

The plutonium-packed question sucker punched him in the gut. The temperature in the room skyrocketed. He tugged at the neck of his sweater.

"Let's take your questions to the gazebo out back."

"Or Odell's Ice Cream Parlor in old town. They've introduced their seasonal flavors and refurbished the outdoor seating area."

Um. "It's pretty cold out."

"That's what coats are for."

"Then, too public. People might start talking."

"What would they say?"

"That you and I are, you know, together."

"That wouldn't be the worst news I've heard."

His throat closed as she ever-so-methodically twined their worlds together.

"Listen, I've got a guy coming out to service some equipment shortly. But tomorrow, I'll be checking in on a program graduate who lives near Rose View Point, north of the lake above the cliffs." Sebastian gave the back of his head a scratch to relieve a fake itch. "If you come along, you and I can stop at the Point afterwards for a Q&A. Take in the view."

High, high above the all-seeing eyes of the town gossipers—though he'd invited the mother of them all to feast on his ego. But the invite spilled out before he could tamp it down.

Digging a hole, man.

But nothing in him demanded he redirect the trajectory of this conversation. If anything, he was inclined to let the course of emotion take him where it led.

"I'd like that very much," she said.

Edging close as he dared, he'd all but turned her need to inquire into an excursion with the only woman who had the capacity to run him aground.

After Sebastian satisfied himself that the Rose's latest graduate of the residential program was amply supplied, still employed, and remained of sound mind, he returned with Marla to his Land Cruiser.

He started the engine. "You won't get very far at Rose View Point wearing heels."

"I thought ahead." Grinning, Marla wiggled a pair of athletic shoes in pristine condition and slipped them on. "Our date called for proper footwear."

"Date?"

"Isn't it?"

"I'm only helping you do your job."

"Up close and personal."

He froze.

The fire in her gaze melted his resolve to feel nothing for her into a slushy puddle.

She regarded him with intrigue. "Do I scare you?"

Yes. "No."

She returned a cheeky grin. "I wouldn't be offended if you said yes."

"Falling in love scares me."

"Is that even a possibility?"

No! "Yes."

Up went her brows. "Now I really have questions."

In no time, they'd reached the northern end of Wild Rose Ridge and drove in silence toward the elevation marking Rose View Point.

At the summit, a swift wind needled through Sebastian's jacket as he led them to the observation deck built into an outcropping. A grand view of the choppy lake sprawled below them.

At the wood railing, she shivered.

He set his arm around her shoulders and rubbed his hand along her arm in effort to draw warmth.

She curled to his side and emitted a soft moan of ecstasy.

Chills tingled inside his chest at the satiny feel of her hair against his skin. Even if she were bald—and she nearly was—he only saw beauty.

The thought of her being unattached and alone unnerved him. Protective instincts roared.

This giant of a personality known by all felt small and vulnerable beside him. In that fleeting moment, he thought he would take a bullet for her. Even if she were the one who pulled the trigger.

"So, back to yesterday's question. It makes no sense to me why you're still single."

He raised a section of her hair over her ear, playfully fingered her collarbone, and felt nimbly along her ribs. "You aren't armed with any hidden recording devices, are you?"

Unleashing an infectious giggle, she shook her head and doubled forward.

He'd always enjoyed the melody of her laugh. Had wanted to be the reason for it. Sadly, he had been. Only he was the object of ridicule among their peers, Marla the ringleader.

"Cut it out! I'm ticklish!" she squealed.

"I'll have to add that to my list of fascinating facts about Marla."

She sat upright like a flag up a pole. A dumbstruck expression came to her gaze and shifted hungrily over his.

In an entertaining game of make-believe, she wielded an air mic and slipped into reporter persona. "I'm here at an undisclosed locale with Mr. Sebastian Monroe, Director of the Rose of Sharon Rescue Mission. Inquiring minds want to know why you, a gorgeous *and* intelligent man, are still single."

She moved the air-mic near his mouth.

What he remembered of the Himalayan summit shrank to an elevation of three inches compared to this location … with this woman … her words a balm.

"My work doesn't lend itself to staying in one spot. Makes starting a family a challenge."

Okay, that was a blatant lie. A family would be the bedrock of his success. He'd witnessed countless examples over the years of men buoyed by the involvement of their wife—and kids, if a man were so blessed.

"Interesting factoid. You want a wife, a family?"

"An intact one. Built to withstand conflict and opposition."

Bringing a hand near his mouth, he played her game of reporter-subject. "Miss Mavis, I have it on authority that you were determined to be married by the time you turned thirty. You're thirty-one."

A brittle grin appeared. "I came close. But he—my ex-fiancé—changed his mind."

A hot breath pressed against his ribs. He curled his hand into a fist.

No man leaves Marla Mavis!

Her gaze went glassy and distant as if unlocking a vault of dark memory. She bent to pluck a weed that snaked through the planks and released it to the wind. "It doesn't take a rocket scientist to connect the dots between 'I have cancer' and 'I've had a change of heart.'"

Sebastian had learned about Marla's breast cancer diagnosis through a social worker friend at the hospital in Ellensburg, but this painful fact of a broken engagement hadn't reached him.

Given her role at the *Observer*, she must have gone to great extremes to keep the news under wraps.

If she'd only given him more consideration in high school ... cared enough to know his heart … the real reason he'd been dozing at his desk.

"My ex contacted me recently," she said. "He wants a chance to talk about what happened."

"Did you tell him no way, no how?"

She lifted a shoulder. "I'm weighing the cost-benefit of letting him explain."

Fury thundered. "Whoever this guy is, he's not worthy of you."

She rewarded him with a smile and gave his arm a dismissive little press that could have catapulted him to the moon.

"You heap compliments when you really don't know me."

Her tone hinted at a need to be known beyond the public persona. What she didn't know was that he'd never tired of studying her complexities—and not for lack of effort.

"You were raised by a single mom as boldly determined and independent as you are but, unlike you, she lost her battle with cancer. Last fall, you were ticketed for speeding."

She gawked at him. "How could you possibly know that?"

"Officer Ford Huntley."

A huff. "I was running late to the Bradshaw rodeo to scoop national news anchors after Walker Bradshaw rode that killer bull."

Yes, that top story had reached Sebastian.

Bradshaw's death-defying ride resulted in the bull rider's retirement, a brave decision he made for the sake of his dream girl.

Sebastian pressed a finger to his palm. "Your go-to

inspirational quote is 'You may see me struggle, but you will never see me quit.'"

Palpable intrigue came to her eyes and colored them the shade of a hidden meadow drenched in sunlight.

"Those words … they sustained me through treatments."

Words Sebastian had written to Marla when she got the fantastic news of an all-clear. Because learning that she'd celebrated alone … the sound of her choking sobs on the other side of the door … undid him.

"Your readership for Marla's Musings has grown significantly since its inception."

"The Observer doesn't publish those numbers."

"They'll leak stats if you know the right people."

Her bemused smile intensified. "Is there anyone you don't know?"

"I still haven't met Rose Arrington. Pastor Michael said her husband Jon welded the rose arch near Beach Park."

"Easy fix. Take one of Rose's adult barre classes with me."

"This isn't my home," he said, bluntly.

"The rescue mission will unravel under someone else's management. You can't leave these people. They adore you!"

"It's not their opinion that drives me, Marla. It's yours."

At this juncture, Marla could have retreated. Sebastian steeled himself against the blow of rejection.

Instead, she moved closer and shifted a furrowing gaze over his, unifying their paths.

Her chest heaved and breaths went jagged and hot.

A high voltage current surged through Sebastian's limbs and rendered him momentarily catatonic.

Need teetered on an unrecoverable precipice. Self-control drained from Sebastian's body. He ached to kiss those fiery red lips and claim her for himself.

To have and to hold and to protect her, always and forever.

Marry me, Marla!

Far too often—and from a safe distance—he'd imagined what this experience might be like. His imagination had come up woefully short. Reality begged for more of her.

"Do you ever wish you could take back something you said?"

Marla's question lowered the boil of passion to a simmer.

"Off the record?"

She nodded rapidly, evoking his vulnerability.

"I've wished I'd spoken up when I had the chance." His confession eked out like a teenage boy whose voice was changing.

Man, she did crazy things to his brain.

She tilted her head to the side and deepened her gaze. "Have you ever written something you regret?"

Where was she going with this? Skepticism niggled and defenses reared back. "I regret not writing more.

Thank you notes, letters of commendation. That sort of thing."

A whimsical muse wandered over her face. "I regret that you and I didn't date in high school. You would have been good for me. Who knows, we may have had something really special."

Spoken as though the opportunity had come and gone, vanishing like a vapor.

But if she saw no future with him, he at least needed her to know … "Never settle for less than what you're worth."

Fool, for exposing his heart! But if he didn't offer it now, he never would.

Heavenly light came to her face as though she'd traveled through the stratosphere, encountered the divine, and slingshot her way back to him.

"How can anyone know what they're worth?" she said, feebly.

"You're worth the cost of a man's life."

"Don't be ridiculous. No one would die for me."

"Jesus did. He considers you his favorite."

"The planet holds an estimated population of eight billion people, and you boldly claim that the God who created them all likes me best?"

"Yes."

Her lids flickered and her tone thinned. "That's the most profound and romantic thing I have ever heard. Your words outclass Shakespeare."

She moistened her lips and tipped them in invitation.

Man, he wanted to kiss her. His pulse jackhammered behind his ears, a sure and certain indication of doom.

Ardor marked her features and elongated the smile

lines aside her eyes. “May I quote you, Mr. Monroe, the Rose of Sharon’s show-stopping, capable director?”

All the reasons why he should never have let his heart romp around in her realm returned in a cruel, endless loop of headline news, the catty western North Carolinian reporter gulping down their misfortune.

Top Story! City Manager Hugh Monroe’s estate destroyed by fire. Local agencies rally to meet needs of the family, though despondency over the loss and blame shifting contributed to the breakup of the mayor’s marriage. Wife relinquishes custody over twin sons, Benedict and Sebastian.

Each sentence a staple gun to his ego.

He shoved the charcoaled images aside and created space. “Never use my name.”

A pout.

He rallied, dared to steady her shoulders, and lasered his stare. “Promise me, Marla.”

She hesitated before responding in a slow, methodical nod that felt in every way like Sebastian may have opened the gates of hell and thrown away the key.

Chapter Six

The following morning, Marla reviewed Conklin's ghost-written draft of the quarterly. To her happy surprise, she found his writing far more engaging than she'd presumed. And wasn't it her propensity for hasty, unsubstantiated judgment what hurt Sebastian years ago?

She emailed the document back to Conklin with editorial notes and fought to concentrate on her own article, due first to Lorraine in less than two weeks. But yesterday's informative outing with Sebastian arm-wrestled with today's effort to make progress.

When the earth-trembling shift in their working relationship was a kiss away, he was all elbows.

A poignant backstory hovered behind his guarded gaze. She must discover it! Knowing the circumstances that shaped him would add depth and significance to an otherwise dull news item.

The cheery ping of her phone alarm brought her to her feet. "Time to volunteer."

What would she find Sebastian doing? Playing board games with the guests? Listening with all ears to their stories? Splitting wood for the hearth? Finding a cure for cancer?

He was Marla's cure.

But if lousy men hadn't stuck around in her life, why should she entertain the possibility that Sebastian, a good man, would?

Before leaving the *Observer,* Marla stepped into Cilly's office to allay her concern about deadlines. She found the testy news director fingering through a file cabinet.

"Tell me you are making progress with the article," Cilly said, dryly.

"It's taking shape. I'll have it to Lorraine for edits by the 25th of March. In fact, I'm off to put in my hour of service and gather more data."

"At this point, online research would be a more efficient use of your time."

"But neglecting to put faith in action won't help the homeless, now will it."

How about that? She was thinking and acting like a humanitarian.

Like *him*.

It was common knowledge that one was influenced by the company they kept. Marla very much liked who she was becoming in Sebastian's company.

From Marla's vantage point inside the front entry of the Rose of Sharon, she was rewarded to see Sebastian in the dining hall with a little girl in his arms.

"You and Carlie are looking well," he said, addressing the woman beside him.

"Thanks to you, Mr. Monroe. We were desperate when we got here."

"Proud of you."

Sebastian rotated the child toward the woman, but the girl squealed a retort and clung to his neck. He gave the girl a winning smile, quieting her in a therapeutic manner that sent rivers of molten chocolate through Marla's body.

What hope did Marla have if even little girls had no defense against his charms?

Taking the child from Sebastian's hold, the woman thanked him again.

When they reached the threshold, Marla graced mother and child with a smile.

The woman pressed her little girl near her heart. "No matter your predicament, Ma'am, Mr. Monroe will move heaven and earth to see that you have what you need. Carlie and me are living proof."

"Yes. I … thank you."

The more time Marla invested in Sebastian's satiating life of service, the broader her vision and the hungrier her heart became to serve. But she'd be no good for anybody if she didn't forget yesterday's almost-kiss and launch the conversation into a level of superficiality.

Otherwise, she'd ravage him.

The smell of today's lunch clung to the air. "Pizza from Crusty's?" Marla said.

"Smart woman."

"Why not treat your clients to Ben's Seafood and Grille on the river walk?"

"Crusty's will donate."

"Yes, but I could put in a call to Ben's proprietor Bryan J. Carlyle, the celebrity chef out of New Orleans." Marla pulled up his contact information on her phone. "If I can't reach him, I'll call his wife Adelyn. According to their socials and his YouTube cooking channel, they've put muscle in their marriage by championing causes to alleviate hunger."

"To the food insecure, pizza is a feast." He planted his hand against the wall as though hemming her in. "Particularly if it's served with love."

Love. The word fell like a grenade at her feet.

When her ex backpedaled out of the relationship, she vowed not to fall in love again. That way, she would never suffer loss. But Sebastian's steady presence and empowering words chiseled at her vow.

She was a willow. He was a sequoia.

"What is today's top priority?"

Marla nearly lost sight of Sebastian who led her to a walk-in pantry where he commenced loading dry goods and paper products into large cardboard boxes.

He taped the top shut, scribbled a notation alongside it, scooted the box her direction, and handed her a black marker. "Every Friday, we collect a weekend's worth of supplies and deliver them to select recipients in remote locations."

"To their residence?"

"If they have one, yes."

"And if they don't?"

He winked at her and leaned close. "Then we meet them where they are."

She gulped. Her heart somersaulted.

Good grief! Was the man simply incapable of not fanning flames of romance—even in a dry goods pantry?

Marla uncapped the marker. "Who receives this one?"

"The Klein family."

And on and on they worked in tandem, taping and marking, taping and marking.

He told jokes.

She laughed.

He filled boxes.

She labeled them.

Time lost all constraints.

The alarm on her cell sounded, hailing her maximum hour of service to the community had come to a blaring end.

Disappointment lengthened the lines aside his eyes. "Time for you to head out?"

Mercy, no! They'd developed a seamless, instinctual team mentality. She did not want to leave. Filling cardboard boxes with canned soup and protein bars alongside Sebastian Monroe—Rose of Sharon's interim director passing through town—was undiluted heaven.

She set the annoying alarm to snooze. "I can make time."

To let herself feel anything more for him was unequivocally the greatest mistake her heart could make. One look at her marred body and he would regret his decision.

But even if Sebastian claimed he was blind to the obvious, how could she trust that he was being honest?

Even so, would he ever forgive her for the way she'd treated him? How carelessly she'd misjudged him and led others to believe he would never amount to anything. Such ignorance!

Could Sebastian learn to love the woman she was becoming, the Marla after cancer? The one determined to rewrite her story and give God the credit for sustaining her through suffering?

In order for Marla to redirect public opinion and publish something meaningful, she couldn't keep Sebastian's name out of it. He was what a remarkable story was to the reader who needed its message—the reason her piece could capture the hearts of her readership.

"How's your article coming along?"

There he went, utilizing his supernatural ability to read her thoughts. It unnerved her as much as she relished it.

"Poorly, considering you've only shared little dribbles of information and refuse to let me credit you for your efforts to rescue the rescue mission." Pleased with herself at the catchy comment, she smiled big teeth. "Readers crave irony."

A random fantasy filled the chamber of Marla's imagination, one where Sebastian sacrificed all to save the day … and pursued the girl who'd insulted him, smelling of undying love and looking like a remarkable happy ending.

Top story! Top story!

Another wide swipe of the packing tape over the box screeched at Sebastian's firm pull. "A romance columnist covering a topic that is anything but romantic. There's your irony."

He slid another box her direction and collected more items from the shelf.

She wrote the recipient's name on the box. "I did finally happen upon one item of interest. Your work in Bangladesh. What was that about?"

The cell alarm hailed another nine minutes had passed.

"We'll start simple," she said, snoozing the alarm.

A troubled brow darkened his countenance. The dangling light bulb flickered off, then on.

"Meaning easy, not stupid."

For Pete's sake, Sebastian Monroe was far from stupid. Here was her chance to restore what her words had broken. "The truth is, you're brilliant, Seb."

A ravenous hunger filtered into his gaze haloed by a heady golden glow.

"Your good looks, muscle, and kind heart aren't essential to manage this place, but they sure are an added bonus."

He stood ten feet taller as though feasting on her respect.

She served more portions. "I was entirely wrong about you in high school. I'd like us to be friends. *Good* friends."

Disenchantment rang in his eyes.

"Or … more."

She may just as well have cut out her heart and served it to him on a platter.

Driving a hard left, he popped the confetti bubble over her head by steering the conversation to the safe zone of a Third World country.

"You asked about my work in Bangladesh," he said. "The people are vulnerable to natural disasters. I was involved in building infrastructure and training at the community level to look for early warning systems. How to recover more readily when the inevitable happens."

"What software systems did you use to measure progress?"

Another hard swipe of the tape echoed off the walls. He yanked the jagged edge to cut the end and ran a hand over the top. “My job was to show up and do the work. Progress enough.”

Chiseling through his outer shell to get to the meaty stuff was akin to carving marble with a marshmallow.

“But using objective measures would ensure that what you’re doing is significant.”

“I can feel it in my heart and see the effect in people’s faces.” He slid another taped box her direction. “The Nancy Jaynes family.”

Taking the pungent marker, she jotted down the name.

He nodded to communicate accuracy as though these supplies reaching their intended destination were tantamount to ensuring astronauts returned safely back to earth. He hefted the load onto a dolly, fitting it levelly alongside the others.

“Two more, and we’ll be ready to deliver these.”

Deliver them? She had a schedule to keep, an article to shore up. Cecilia’s antennae were already raised at the inordinate amount of time Marla spent on location rather than at her desk.

“I really need to get back to the office. You’ll have to ask Oscar or Leonard to lend a hand.”

“It’s you I want.”

Sebastian’s evocative offer swirled like decadent fudge and tasted like bliss. And really, what better way for Marla to gather rich, relatable content than to walk in his shoes.

He hefted a crate from a pallet to a shelf as though it

weighed a feather. The strength and agility of his movements stirred her senses.

Oscar entered. “Hi, Miss Mavis.” He passed a clipboard to Sebastian, handed him a pen. “Need your John Hancock on the inventory ledger, Bash.”

Sebastian did so.

Again, Marla concentrated her gaze on Sebastian’s unique, illegible signature. He’d make a superb physician.

The next alarm ping was followed by a call from Lorraine. Marla silenced them both. Roving reporters roved, and her subject had finally opened up. At this juncture, she’d not be hindered.

“You coming with me?” he said.

“Wouldn’t miss it.”

“Community service sure looks good on you.”

Sebastian’s lop-sided grin razzed her senses. His eyes communicated more than a simple explanation could give. His gaze traveled in zig-zag formation beyond her outer wall and into her soul.

Searching, wondering, admiring her.

“I never realized how beautiful your eyes are,” he said, directly. “Some parts green, some parts blue. Nice.”

“You’d have to really care enough about someone to study the color of their eyes.”

“I do care. Always have. I told you as much at the Point.”

Her lids shuddered a few times. What to make of his soul-stirring statement?

“What you really need is a girlfriend,” she blurted.

With force, Sebastian stuffed a case of paper products onto the shelving unit like an agitated parent putting a kid in timeout.

Yes, she'd tripped a wire but if there was any possibility he had considered her remotely qualified to be his girlfriend, this was his chance to say so.

"Now, list characteristics of your ideal woman and, once this article is published, I'll collaborate with my search team and see who we can find."

He leaned a lazy arm over the crate and interlaced his fingers. His voice went husky and irresistible. "My ideal wife—"

"I said woman."

"I said wife."

"Then, um, go on."

"I want a wife who's persistent and goes after what she wants but is sensitive enough to discern if her determination might railroad someone else's dreams. Someone who's faced adversity with grace and would willingly serve alongside me, sharing her own story to empower others."

"You, you've given this future wife some thought."

Closer now … "Someone who's unhindered by obstacles and sees her differences as opportunities for growth. A wildflower in a rose garden."

Sebastian's arrangement of words, the smooth tone of his voice when they left his lips, sizzled hot down her limbs. She tamped down a firestorm of emotion.

"One who's about—" He placed his wide palm on the top of her head. "This tall."

Her alarm chimed. Silence!

"Work can wait a little longer."

He winked. "Let's go deliver some love together."

Chapter Seven

Yesterday's daring description of Marla—combined with the way she reveled in their joint service to the community—upped Sebastian's difficulty of leaving.

She had always been the one he wanted. The want had grown to a need he couldn't reconcile against a greater opportunity. Was he wrong to insist God use him in a larger capacity, all the while dodging the unforgiving media?

Maybe. But, at long last, a viable candidate to replace Sebastian appeared in his inbox.

Judging from the profile photo, Roger was a seasoned veteran on mission fields all over the globe. Happily married, flexible, and experienced. The references Sebastian contacted were solid and promising. After a lengthy conversation, Sebastian found Roger equally impressive over the phone.

But the thrill of an answer to prayer didn't align with the quaking of his heart.

A lead ball formed in his gut at the prospect of living geographically far from Marla. The red-haired lioness of the media may not be as fiercely independent as he'd presumed. She aroused his senses in ways he could no longer ignore. She was the standard by which he'd measured other potential women.

None measured up.

Was Sebastian an idiot to hold the girl of his heart at a distance because she represented the media? When had he allowed fear a greater voice than wisdom and common sense? Had he done the work God prepared for *him* to accomplish—in the place where God intended … for as long as it took?

And did that work include a future with her?

"How soon can you get here, Roger?" Sebastian said, his tone teetering on desperation.

"Tomorrow, if you've got the time."

Saturday. The most demanding day of the week. "Plenty of time."

And, *oh,* he'd hear no end of rebuke from Hilda over this.

Saturday at noon, Sebastian met Roger at a charter plane airstrip in Wild Rose Ridge. From there, they drove to the Rose of Sharon where Roger met the small but mighty staff.

Heading into town, they drove past undulating folds of fruitful wineries and buzzing commerce that ringed the iconic rose-shaped lake. Cruise ships docked in the marina in preparation for tourist season. Vacation homes were tucked in the hillsides.

Sebastian had become so hyper-focused on achieving his goal to revive the Rose of Sharon that he'd overlooked how much the Ridge had grown in population, vibrancy, commerce, and wealth since he lived here.

The wealthy sect of the town could sustain the Rose and its ancillary programs if more of them were aware. Marla and her article were the key.

Could he trust Marla to use her words responsibly this time?

If Sebastian took this dream job, he'd have achieved his own brand of success. But in Marla's eyes, he'd be an utter failure to walk away at this juncture. It would give him no rest.

But what if he sacrificed his dream to manage the mission and failed anyway?

God, I need discernment.

Sebastian parked at the civic center to meet commercial realtor Diana Alexander. According to Benedict, Diana was an influential member of city council and insisted on being the one to conduct a tour of the area. She and the Schulte sister cohorts, Barbara and Lorraine, had also baked an outstanding homemade lasagna.

Avoiding direct answers to Diana's side questions about his relationship with Marla took the skill of a criminal defense attorney.

At the museum, Sebastian found himself riveted to the curator's recollection of Wild Rose Ridge's proud beginnings—the legendary and factual accounts. During high school, Sebastian had no interest in learning about the town's intriguing history. He'd grabbed his hard-earned diploma and had run.

At tour's end, Sebastian introduced Roger to key

retailers and benefactors. Among them, the bookshop where Roger met Benedict who *shocker!* instantly closed the book he was reading, made eye contact, and proffered a hand.

This was going exceedingly well.

Back outside, savory scents from the river walk a block east of Main Street drew Sebastian to Ben's Seafood and Grille. An effective strategy for reeling Roger into making the Ridge his home was to get him hooked on the finest restaurants in town. And since Marla had spoken highly of Ben's, Sebastian couldn't go wrong.

Marla. That beautiful woman was with him even when she wasn't. Unbidden, his love for Marla had grown to an insatiable hunger.

Soon after Sebastian and Roger were seated, the waitstaff brought a steamy basket of French bread and took their orders.

Roger smoothed a pat of butter on his bread. "What led you to serve in the Ridge?"

"One of the pastors in town is a friend of mine. He contacted me about the need for a director. Since Benedict and I lived here during high school, it made sense to fill the role. Interim director."

"From what I've observed, you've gained some ground in a short amount of time, given limited resources. You've garnered the support of influential people, which is no small task. I'm not confident I could fill your shoes."

"You are more than qualified."

Through the front door, Marla entered, all smiles.

His heart leapt to see her with an unfamiliar guy. Strong, virile, with foxy intentions in his gait.

Was this a date? It couldn't be a date. Was it?

Sebastian had failed to turn her head, apparently. A better man had stoked her interest. Why had he thought she'd ever give him any serious consideration?

Man, he needed out of this lash-up quickly, but jealousy coiled and hissed.

Roger's voice faded as Sebastian's concentration funneled Marla's direction.

The guy fawned over her. A slick devil in his tailored suit and gleaming Italian loafers. The bearing of royalty and privilege who sported razor sharp lines and teeth like a shark.

A successful type with money to burn. He could probably purchase the country of her choosing. What a difference this man's money could make if he wasn't presently wasting it at an expensive restaurant—escorting the girl Sebastian had wanted for himself as they cut through the dining area.

Never mind that Sebastian and Roger would soon be enjoying their own overpriced entrees—food enough to feed his clients for several days.

Hypocrite!

Seated at a private corner table, Marla smiled at something the guy said.

In response, he kissed her hand.

Sebastian's pulse raced. He hated this guy!

Roger's rasping cough yanked Sebastian back to attention.

"Mr. Monroe, you look like you've seen a ghost."

Haunted by a past he couldn't outrun.

A familiar lament stabbed at his ego. He would never be adequate enough for Marla Mavis.

When their plates were served, Sebastian took his fork

and pierced the blackened salmon laying limp on a bed of rice. His stomach clenched.

He drained the water from his glass, set it down, and honed his attention back on Roger. "Go on. You were saying?"

"I wasn't. When your gaze drifted, I paused. Figured you were giving my concerns some thought."

Way to impress!

"Concerns, Sir?"

Roger methodically dotted his mouth with a linen napkin and lagged a glance away.

The volume of babbling patrons increased. Jazz music screeched from corner speakers. The smell of seafood choked.

A giggle in Marla's corner ratcheted up to the chest-pounding reverberation of a death metal concert.

Sebastian's blood boiled.

Censure snaked over Roger's bushy brow. "I don't believe this is where the Lord has called me."

What? No!

The booth shrank around him. "I believe he has."

A tic moved along Roger's jaw. "Do you question my judgment?"

"No, no. Sir. It's just, I've got another offer and need someone to replace me as soon as possible," he said, flatly.

"Filling a ministry role can't be rushed for the sake of convenience."

"I realize that, but it's possible that you've misinterpreted what God has said."

"I'm more inclined to believe it's you who isn't listening." Roger placed his bunched napkin over his entree in a show of absolution. "It would be disobedient for me to interfere with work that God has clearly assigned to someone else."

If Sebastian were honest, he had feared how the next director would handle the waves of support that might result from Marla's article. More importantly … would the next director care enough to learn the names of those who passed through the mission's doors? Would they shepherd well and mobilize the Outreach Team to invite the homeless in for hot meals, showers, and safety? Would they make sure and certain that clients were offered practical solutions to overcome their predicament?

Would they follow up with program graduates? … Check in with Gus and his dog Piper?

Would Marla stop serving after he left? Hers were the best volunteer hands the mission had ever known—and far more effective when their hands served together.

Sebastian's voice went ruthlessly level, but strained. "I … I can't stay here."

Roger's expression morphed to that of a sage father who knew better.

Within the shadows of Marla's table, her date sat back with a start as though she'd slapped him.

Tension amplified. The environment turned thorny.

Mr. Foxy massaged his temples, shook his head disdainfully, then drained his cocktail like it was punch.

If anyone could drive a guy to drink, it was Marla.

When Foxy stood and stepped away from the table, Marla's expression paled to match the linen and read one part desperation and two parts rage.

Was this guy going to leave her there? No one leaves Marla Mavis in the corner!

Sure as shooting, Marla's date smoothed a hand over his tie as though wiping his hands of her.

Sebastian's ears pricked at the guy's pathetic voice.

"I'm sorry, Marla. It was a mistake for me to give this another go."

"This? Mistake?" she fumed, gnashing at his caustic word choices.

"Don't get me wrong. You're more beautiful than ever, especially without that wig, and I'm grateful you're well now, but the fact that you might get sick again? I … I don't know."

"What don't you know?" she bit back.

"I thought I could handle it, but it still scares me. I'm really sorry."

Leaving Roger time to ponder his decision regarding the job, Sebastian fired to his feet.

Instantly, he found himself at Marla's table, intercepting Foxy's retreat.

The meddlesome guy bent his arms in defense and hooded his brow.

"You're on a date," Sebastian pressed, widening his feet.

"I was. Now I'm not."

"A man doesn't leave a woman alone like that. Most definitely not Marla." *My Marla!*

"How I handle my affairs is none of your business, chump."

Sebastian bowed his chest. "Everyone in this town is my business."

"Who are you, the mayor? 'Cause you sure don't look like one." Foxy laughed and adjusted the knot of his tie.

Swiftly, Marla came to Sebastian's side. Using his

shoulder as a barrier, she gripped Sebastian's arm. "The mayor wouldn't have a town worth governing if it weren't for Sebastian Monroe's involvement, you selfish jerk."

Sebastian's heart smiled. Then he said, "You do realize that Marla Mavis is one of the most public and influential women in this town with the power to destroy your reputation?"

Foxy ran a scathing glance down the front of Sebastian's frame. "Looks like she may have already done a number on yours."

Every molecule of self-control and sound mind and compassion threatened to drain from Sebastian's body. His fingers opened and closed, opened and closed, itching to take a swing.

"I should deck you right here, right now."

Foxy scoffed.

Sebastian came within inches and spoke through clenched teeth. "If you ever come anywhere near Marla again, I won't hesitate, pal."

In a flash, Foxy shoved his hands against Sebastian's chest with force enough to send him stumbling into the waitstaff behind him.

Their feet tangled. Sebastian crashed to his side.

Wine and seafood entrees slid off the circular serving tray and scatted over the floor.

A cacophony of horrified gasps echoed off the wood paneled walls.

"Maybe things will work out for us some day in the future," Foxy said to Marla with a shrug of false optimism.

"Don't hold your breath. I won't be available," Marla sniped.

Her rebuke sent Foxy out the door.

Sebastian rolled to his back. The light blinded. He smelled like he'd been washed ashore. Probably looked it too.

Marla came to Sebastian's side, her face a silhouette against the back light. She drew a hand to her throat. "What … what was that all about?"

"Defending your honor."

Ruining my life in the process.

Great. Sebastian had failed on two counts.

The impulsive decision to provoke the wrath of a complete stranger—one dripping with power and influence—would be headline news by tomorrow morning. That and he had no successor.

Roger, a perfect and timely candidate, respectfully declined the job and left the over-priced entree untouched. The mission (aka Sebastian) would bear the weight of the bill.

He'd lose his dream job and be stuck in one spot. But if God called him to live the life of a sacrificial lamb, what better reason than to do it for the sake of the woman he loved—the woman he could no longer stand to live without.

Marry Me, Marla!

Time to be brave and let her know he wanted to be the reason she would no longer be available, as she'd so brashly claimed.

The rabid hush in the restaurant see-sawed his ego.

Marla's touch on his arm flushed adrenaline through his body.

Back on his feet, he took full notice of her appearance now. She donned a velvety crimson dress and heels that accented firm legs. Her shimmery hair was styled all fancy like she'd invested her life savings on this evening. Hoping to win the affection of a loser.

Sebastian was no better. Some role model.

Still, she took his hands and squeezed. Her eyes watered and her voice went desperate. "You protected my dignity. I love you for that."

He must tell her he loved her!

Throaty murmurs rumbled throughout the room. Eyeballs finger-pricked at his skin.

"I care about you."

Lame, but Sebastian's courage scampered off too quickly.

"Let's get out of here."

She nodded consent.

Without a word, he escorted Marla to his car and drove to Rosehill Community Church grounds. The panoramic view over the town at dusk afforded them a secluded elevation and a place to sit.

He led her through the prominent steel rose gate outside the main entrance and along the flagstone steps to the prayer garden.

If ever Sebastian wanted to invite God's presence, now was the time—in a spot dedicated to prayer.

A variety of shrubs and flowering bushes were beginning to blossom along the wrought-iron fence encasing the garden. They sat on a lone granite bench with an exceptional view of the lake.

The remains of sunlight traced patches of striated clouds in a golden amber.

Gently, Sebastian moved a hand to massage Marla's neck. "Was that the man who broke off your engagement?"

"Yes."

"What made him bolt this time?"

Her lower lip curled between her teeth. She fidgeted with her sleeve. "I told him that I could not guarantee my cancer wouldn't return with a vengeance at some point."

The weight of her sorrow made sucking sounds in his chest.

"You don't deserve to be treated like that," Sebastian said, tenderly. "No one does. I'm sorry."

She could barely nod.

"People didn't know you when you were open-hearted and brave and invincible in high school. I think you're amazing."

"You wouldn't say that if you saw my scars."

"Putting words in my mouth again."

She regarded him keenly.

"We all have scars—physical, emotional. Even Jesus, who chose to keep his. They invite people to be curious about our stories and how we endured suffering. Like that hook in a story that invites the reader to know more."

The cold air whisked past, twirling the ends of her hair, moving like strawberry syrup over the collar of her ivory coat.

"I don't deserve your kindness." Her posture and tone took on a ferocious strength. "I was judgmental and ignorant in high school. If I'd known the truth about you, I would have written something entirely different."

"Like what?"

"You're the most desirable, successful person I have ever met."

Chapter Eight

Yearning for Marla mounted and roared. Sebastian's heart tumbled and fell and surrendered. If he didn't take a risk ... if he hid behind fear a moment longer …

"I want to kiss you, Marla."

Her lashes fluttered interest. Hot breaths thickened between them.

Slowly, she lifted her chin in consent. Passion throbbed in her hazy eyes.

He ran his hands along her cheeks.

Her chest rose and fell.

He brought his lips to hers—feathery and soft.

She responded in feverish hunger and wound her arms around his neck, pulling him nearer.

The rhythm of their kisses was deep and wild and cadenced, a well-rehearsed dance.

He led, and she followed for what felt like centuries.

Way more gratifying than he'd imagined.

Eventually, she pulled back, taking a sharp influx of air.

The tug of resistance equaled the opposing force of two magnets when pulled apart against their design. The unnatural feeling left him powerless.

He drew in air and assessed her.

She rewarded him with a smile. "I'm falling for you."

"I fell for you years ago."

Her brows lifted. "You are one patient man."

"My patience is running out."

"Don't leave me."

"I'm still here."

"No, I mean, stay with me … here in the Ridge."

Ethereal threads of evening light illuminated Sebastian's naturally rugged features. A halo effect encircled his head, making him more distinctly angelic.

"When news of what you're doing here reaches people, you'll have more volunteers and food donations than you can handle."

Sebastian's gaze trailed ahead as though summoned by angels, seeking their counsel. Or retreating at the speed of a cheetah.

Had Marla come on too strong? Read too much into this moment? Translated that white-hot kiss into a marriage proposal?

Maybe Sebastian shared her ex's fear of being a widower and needed to back out before it was too late.

Oh my, her heart was in trouble!

He loosened his hold. “Knowing how I feel about you, I had hoped you wouldn’t go forward with that article … especially if you cite me as primary source.”

“I have to, Sebastian. We’ll both benefit.”

“Then it was wishful thinking on my part.”

“Please believe me when I say, I would never print anything negative.” And here it went. “I no longer want to be just friends. I love you.”

A smoky expression marked his features. “I’ve always loved you, Marla.”

“Then you have to trust me. This is my opportunity to un-do the mess I made years ago.”

At that, he jerked back. The atmosphere shifted like tectonic plates.

“Sounds to me like your need to include my name is for your own advantage … to relieve your guilt.”

A soul-shuddering darkness collected in Sebastian’s eyes and turned them charcoal.

She was losing him.

“It’s time you came out of hiding and gave the Rose of Sharon the visibility it needs,” Marla said, tenaciously.

He stood and took a step back. “I was wrong to kiss you.”

“I disagree. I believe it’s the smartest decision you’ve made to date.”

“I let my heart get in the way.”

"It's your heart that I'm after—if you'll trust me with it."

He wandered near the fence, glanced over his shoulder at her. "There's more to be done out there."

Enough of this stubbornness. She came to his side and pivoted him to face her. "And plenty of other men God can use to do it."

"I have a job offer waiting for me. Countries I haven't visited."

"The welfare of all humanity is not your responsibility."

Conflict drew the lines of his face tight.

"Did you ever read the news story about a family in western North Carolina whose estate was destroyed by fire?"

She regarded him with probing gaze. "Mom told me something about it when I was about, I don't know, maybe nine or ten."

"It was Benedict's and my childhood home. Twenty-one years ago." He jammed his hands in his pockets. "Local and state organizations intervened to secure housing, provide food and clothing. Helped us rebuild. But the reporter misconstrued facts associated with the fire. She used her position to slander my father's name. Stated that Benedict and I would be orphaned."

"That's awful."

A rueful expression deepened the planes of his cheeks.

"Benedict coped by hiding his heart behind his intellect. A perfect SAT score got him into a university. My brief stent at a local community college only stood in the way of my need to rise above the devastation and give back to the world."

"Then you proved the media's predictions wrong."

Dimming sunlight fell over the ridge line and brushed his shoulders. The rose gold sky darkened to a lonesome blue. Clouds cloaked a smattering of stars.

He turned a tentative gaze on her. "The fire wasn't the problem. It was the way the reporter spun the story … it destroyed my parent's marriage."

Shock waves jarred Marla. No wonder he held media at a distance. Marla was media, then and now. Hence, a threat.

But that kiss ...

She would not give up on what might be her last shot at true love without a fight.

"You have people here who depend on you." She pointed at the ground beneath his boots. "This is your mission field. I want everyone to know about the impact you've had on their lives."

"The work I do isn't about me or my name."

"You act like God will strike you dead if you dare accept credit for all the good things you've done."

"That's not it." His nostrils flared. "I don't—"

She closed in. "You said you loved me, then engaged me in a remarkable kiss session. If the fact that the cancer I had could still make a widower out of you isn't frightening, I can only assume you can't forgive me."

"You're wrong. I forgave you years ago."

"Then you don't trust me."

A tic jumped at his jaw. "I trust you'll write an excellent article, but if my name is in it, we need to end what we started tonight."

A soul-crushing quiet had her swallowing back the boulder in her throat. His image blurred.

The weight of grief pulled at Marla's chin. Loss squeezed around her middle.

With effort, she drew in air. Because the only man who'd been a faithful friend and had bravely voiced his devotion stood inches away but had virtually taken the next flight out of the Ridge—off to better causes than committing to have and to hold a small-town columnist.

Chapter Nine

At what point had Marla let herself get duped into falling for Mr. Wonderful? Make that, Mr. Successful.

Last Saturday, a solemn quiet had accompanied their drive back to town. The atmosphere held the joy of a funeral dirge.

He'd kissed her cheek.

She'd taken one final sniff of his steady presence and coaxed well-wishes.

They parted companionably with no promises that their paths would ever cross.

Clearly, Sebastian feared she'd make a mockery of his name again. A thousand times, no! But this was for the best, wasn't it? It would be unethical for her to guilt-trip him into finishing what that kiss started and demand he make her a higher priority than hungry souls around the globe.

Why did Marla let herself believe for a blush of a second that God would consider her an integral part of the heavenly assignment he'd given Sebastian? That he would bring an honorable man into her life who would love her and ... stay.

Genuine love wouldn't thrive against unreasonable demands and conditions.

All weekend, Marla willed herself to honorably release Sebastian, far from her and the Ridge, but several restless nights of intermittent sobbing left its mark on her face the following Monday.

With barely a tap on Marla's door, Angela strode to the desk past the anemic, wilting rubber plant. "Your email signature to the staff reporters reads Marla Monroe."

Gasp. "A typo."

"It reads like a Freudian autocorrect." Angela quirked a niggling grin before she pivoted back to the door, brushing past Lorraine who entered next.

The sorry rubber plant on life support would serve better as a traffic light.

"Cecilia wants my edits to your piece by tomorrow. No pressure."

Manufacturing a pleasant expression, Marla took a deep influx of air, let it out. "You'll have it by day's end."

"Can't wait to read what you've come up with."

"I've added fresh content, photos, and poignant quotes from the staff and consenting guests."

"And Sebastian?"

All trace of resolve melted into a puddle. "You had to bring him into this."

"Naturally." Lorraine pushed her shoulders back. "And your attempt to pretend you haven't been kissed by Prince Monroe is unconvincing," she said, with no shortage of attitude.

"Why couldn't he have been a fictional hero in a romance novel? I could expel a final satisfying breath and close the book. It would be far easier on my heart."

"Sure, sure. Let others have their happy endings while you go back to the safe zone of publishing their stories."

Emotions wailed. Marla trudged to the window. Icy precipitation pinged against the glass. Signs of spring cowered. Foot traffic on Persimmon Street was sparse.

"Sebastian refuses to let me prove I can be trusted. I'm thinking it might be just as effective to write a generalized overview of the organization."

"I've never known you to be a quitter."

Marla whirled. "I'm not quitting. I'm surrendering to spare what's left of my dignity."

"Okay, then you are free to write the article of your heart—a human interest piece on the Rose of Sharon's director. Cecilia will submit your work to the Hazel Wingate Award. The town will rally resources to benefit the organization. Your goal of rebranding yourself will be achieved."

Right. All was well.

Time would heal.

The cloying emptiness would subside. Wouldn't it?

Her capacity to pretend she didn't long for Sebastian had reached a maximum, her heart a hot air balloon about to burst.

By week's end, Marla would receive the signature ID results from her contact at WRR Sheriff's Department. She could rule out Sebastian as the mysterious card writer.

But there was still the matter of the custom T-shirt.

"I managed to locate a print shop in Ellensburg where

a customer identified as CSM had placed an order for that T-shirt I told you about."

"Oh, really?"

"Yes. It was picked up the day before it appeared in my hospital room."

"I knew Sebastian was the one."

"I can't verify that."

"Mercy, sugar. You believe it was him as much as I do. Why do you suppose he didn't just ship it to you?"

With dramatic flair, Marla brought a hand to her chest. "Because the north star of his heart is set to participate in the work. He wants to take large draughts of what only God can do through him … to live a transcendent life that seeks to be part of something bigger than himself. His impact on this earth will outlast his days. Eternity will tell of his involvement. Stories unending!"

"For the record, you never exhibited this much joy or enthusiasm when you were with what's his name."

A flush of pinkish warmth came to Marla's cheeks.

Lorraine pursed her lips. "I strongly suggest you stop living vicariously through everyone else's stories before your own happy ending jets out of here."

Yes, Marla desperately wanted to be a part of Sebastian's life. But her excuses died a slow death.

"But can you seriously envision me, a hometown kind of girl, meandering from continent to continent with no place to call home?"

"Your home is wherever you and your husband are together. And it isn't really living if the fear of loss costs you the one you love."

Acid had pooled in Sebastian's middle last Friday when Marla grasped him on the arm. A ring of red had come to her eyes. He should never have made it a near impossibility to part ways with her, but he'd found her spirited nature brutally attractive.

He could only have hoped to develop an immunity to her.

It was bad enough that he'd memorized her irresistible scent over the past three weeks. The echoes of her confession of love and feel of her affirmation had saturated his soul and would never leave him.

No man forgets the impact of a woman's respect.

But years from now … the first time he fell short … she would remember how she'd once viewed him. The past would be that one stone that tumbled into a rock slide.

To think he'd rehearsed a proposal in the mirror until he could voice it without faltering …

"Marry me, Marla. Marry me, Marla."

A highly anticipated call from Samaritan's Purse the following Monday spared him further belly aching.

"It's wheels up next week, March 31st. Can my driver expect to receive you at Berlin Brandenburg Airport the following day?"

Ha. April Fool's Day.

"Yeah. Sure. Count on it."

. . .

Lamenting and confused Tuesday afternoon, Sebastian left the mission in his staff's and volunteer's hands to meet Pastor Michael at the fairgrounds, east of town.

Sebastian might be hauling heartbreak in his gear bag over losing Marla, but he sure didn't want to venture into this new opportunity without a pastor's blessing.

The sky cleared from this morning's wintery mix. A strengthening sun flooded the grounds. Brisk, icy winds subsided.

Restless bulls were penned on the opposite side of the arena. Retired bull rider Walker Bradshaw was guest-coaching the high school rodeo team this week while his wife Brooke directed a small film crew to chronicle Walker's life after retirement.

Pastor Michael served as team chaplain.

According to Michael, Brooke had selected the Ridge as the ideal location for last year's debut film—a re-creation of her parents' love story that began in Hollywood and culminated in Wild Rose Ridge. When Brooke hired Walker Bradshaw as her animal handler, the project resulted in her own love story.

Two opposing career paths that overcame their differences and accomplished greater good through ... media.

Sebastian's shoes were caked in patches of slushy mud as they ambled along the exterior fencing.

"Thanks for meeting me," Sebastian said.

"Unconventional spot, but God meets us where we are."

Stopping beside Michael, Sebastian stood shoulder-to-shoulder and brought his foot to the bottom rung of the railing. "Maybe he could clue me in as to where I am."

"Headed out of town from what I hear."

"I told you I'd assist on a temporary basis. God needs me elsewhere."

Walker's sharp correction directed at one of the cocky young cowboys rent the air. A safe distance away, Brooke took nimble side-steps with her camcorder, following the action, motioning to boom operators.

"God needs nothing. But it does us good to get involved in the work he's already doing, friend. To presume otherwise is twisted theology."

"People have done a lot to help me at critical times in my life. Disregarding a need is failure on my part."

"And retreating from the woman you love and publicly fought to defend isn't?"

"Oh, you, uh, heard about that?"

"Word travels around a small town—with or without a newspaper."

Sebastian sighed. "What if I fail Marla?"

"This side of eternity, failure is inevitable. To believe you can dodge that bullet is crazy talk. Worse, you'll end up hating yourself for letting a good thing get away."

"I can't take that risk."

"Love is costly. That's why it's so good."

Love, costly. God, good. Yes, he knew. Still, resistance howled.

"I'd sure hate to think you believe the lie that serving God in the Ridge isn't good enough," Michael said, firmly, steadying his gaze ahead … giving time for the truth to sink into Sebastian and expose dark places.

The list of excuses were losing firepower against Michael's wisdom.

"Success is doing everything I can, wherever I'm able, with the life I've been given."

"Success in kingdom work is doing the thing God puts before us—in your case, trusting the Almighty to guard your reputation when love is on the line."

What was before Sebastian? Wild Rose Ridge and a girl named Marla.

Did it matter? Was it enough?

A penned bull threw his weight against the bucking chute. Walker climbed the rungs and gave the bull rope an upward tug.

The stubborn beast thrashed and butted against the metal.

Walker tugged harder.

The bull ceased the fight.

"Our adequacy comes from God alone. He sees your heart of service and is pleased with the effort, no matter how small. Take Emmanuel, Rosehill's grounds keeper, for example."

"Never heard of him."

"Most people haven't, though they'd sure notice the impact if Emmanuel quit. He works tirelessly on the upkeep of our restored prayer garden, the landscaping, and utilities."

A thriving garden filled with sizzling remnants of Marla's kiss.

"I found Emmanuel polishing the wood pews the other day. His service to me, to the folks at Rosehill is essential."

"Good man to have on your team."

"But he won't ever be remarkable, headline news."

Was that what Sebastian was really after? To be a fail-safe, top story sensation in Marla's mind? He'd stop at nothing for others to experience the power and faithfulness of God's love—food, shelter, the coat off his back. But his heart was glass in Marla's hands.

Could Sebastian trust her not to shatter it again?

She might. But the greatest mistake was to refuse to open his heart to the possibility. Because if he chose to settle down in the spot where his heart broke in the first place, it might be the beginning of the greatest dream he had ever imagined.

He knew enough that God had a reason for denying Sebastian a successor. Sure, Oscar was a respectable placeholder with the heart of a lion, but the mission needed more. *Much* more. And Sebastian didn't want to miss the thrill of tending it.

He couldn't leave.

And if he trusted God to be his competence, he could boldly pursue the formerly red-wigged woman—one of media's best assets.

Maybe it was time he linked arms with the press and took full advantage of the good it could do.

Lord, help me be man enough to let love in and courageous enough to stay.

Chapter Ten

By Tuesday afternoon, Marla had reviewed Glen Conklin's surprisingly excellent final report of swoon-worthy couples. She sure had misjudged his abilities and had communicated as much in person, reinforced her thoughts in an email, cc'd Cilly and Lorraine.

Following that, she left the *Observer* and lumbered into the yarn shop to assist the covert operations of select town matchmakers.

Today's group included Lorraine's sister Barbara, the bird-sized, cantankerous office manager of Rosehill Community Church, and Genevieve's mother, the effervescent Helene Peters. But commercial realtor Diana Alexander, Rose Arrington's mother-in-law, respectfully declined today's gathering. Nothing held greater priority to her than being with her adolescent granddaughter Lindee and Rose and Jon's eight month old son Andrew.

Last year's effort to find a perfect helpmate for bubbly Genevieve had drawn Helene out of the shadows of depression. When love bit Genevieve, she overcame her fear of animals and fell for Dr. Adam Beringer, the local veterinarian.

Admittedly, last summer's opposites attract piece was fun to write, but an undercurrent of melancholy had settled into Marla's bones when it went to press. In the wake of a broken engagement, Marla guarded her heart behind a palisade and held her emotions in such tight reserve no one was the wiser.

Until now.

Barbara and Helene clicked and clacked their needles like seasoned professionals, though neither of them had ever created a wearable garment.

A fit of bickering amplified.

Helene paused her knitting. "I disagree. A man who's secretly loved a woman for years has the agency to hold out hope that the object of his affection will appear in God's good time."

Barbara gave an indignant sniff and lifted her pointed chin a notch. "That may be true in fiction. But this is real life."

"I didn't just roll off a turnip truck—" Helene switched her glance to Marla and brought a smile to her lips. "Aw, great to see you. It's been weeks. No knitting tote?"

"I left it at home this morning."

That and her iPad. Nothing to record the minutes of today's meeting.

"You seem distant."

Far, far away …

Where was Sebastian's job taking him? Marla honestly didn't want to know. Otherwise, she'd stupidly hunt him down and make a fool of herself, groveling at his boots.

Not at all how she'd fantasized a memorable happy ending … if God were to bring her one.

Barbara wagged a needle at Marla. "Rose's adult ballet class will cure whatever ails you."

When Marla published Jon and Rose's blissful romance—a welder and a ballerina—she'd used the bold lead line: A Steel Rose.

"You should treat yourself to one of Leilah's custom jewelry pieces," Helene said. "Ask her to create something to compliment your new head of hair."

Ah, yes. Pastor Michael and Leilah's second chance romance—a story to prod any girl to believe in the impossible. At Sebastian's invitation to sit in on the small group at J. Weaver Chapel, she'd witnessed the miraculous pairing played out in living color.

The women's banter dissipated against the thumps of quiet.

Helene moved her gaze to Barbara. "Hunky cowboy Walker Bradshaw and his city-bred bride make a darling couple, don't they?"

Barbara returned a smile. "From my observations at the fairgrounds earlier today, Walker and Brooke are inseparable."

The planet spun. Marla gripped the nearest chair.

A little wave of Barbara's crepey hand re-oriented Marla's attention. "We are anxious to read what you learned about Sebastian Monroe. Has the endeavor fared well?"

Rotten. "Statistics have been hard to come by, but the lives he's touched are immeasurable."

Priceless. Crucial. Everlasting impact …

"Any prospective women we could match him up with?"

"He doesn't want a girlfriend." Sebastian's distinct description ran through her head again. "He wants a wife."

Helene hitched a brow over brightened gaze.

"I sense that your involvement with Sebastian has been profitable," Barbara said, with entirely too much confidence.

"Don't think I can't detect subtext, you two. Remember, I'm one of you." Marla slumped in a chair between them. "Anyway, he's moving on from here."

Wouldn't they all?

"I suppose a selfless man like Sebastian would find it hard to stay in one place unless otherwise motivated." Helene gave a cheeky grin.

Barbara brandished her needle. "Why, according to my conversation with his brother Benedict the other day, Sebastian once stayed out all night to deliver food and clothing to a family at Rosehill. The father lost his job and the mother was ill. They had seven children and would have despaired otherwise."

Could it have been …?

"The Warren family?" Marla said, timorously.

"Why, yes. Artie Warren was a night-shift factory worker."

Helene gave two crisp tongue clucks. "Poor Sebastian must have been dog tired at school."

"Most certainly," Barbara added. "Benedict said it was the week of final exams."

The photo. Sebastian asleep at his desk during an exam. No wonder!

Marla alternated her gaze between Barbara's lifted

brow and Helene's eye-blinking grin. She dredged up some snark. "Got to hand it to you. Working undercover against me."

"You're so close to the situation, you've lost perspective."

"What's to see?"

"Sebastian. You're the wife he wants."

A hot breath billowed and hollowed Marla's lungs. "Maybe so, but not enough to stick around."

"Because you're dishing up reasons for him to leave, thinking less of yourself. Listening to lies. Guarding against another father wound instead of letting God heal with the truth."

Was she?

"Marla, pardon my directness," Helene said. "But for all the colors a girl could wear, I find it an oddity that you've limited yourself to shades of red."

Out of habit, Marla patted her hair as if to re-center a wig she no longer wore. "It matches my hair."

Helene set a gentle hand on Marla's knee and soaked her voice in nurturing grace. "And red hides the fact that your heart is bleeding."

The truth struck like a comet and knocked Marla out of orbit. Had she been emotionally hemorrhaging?

Treasonous heart.

After her ex called off the engagement, she couldn't let the public see her cry. Then, she'd been given another shot at life. This was happy news.

Happy, happy, happy!

Did Sebastian cry after what she'd done to him, silent and alone? He bore little to no evidence she'd once pummeled his ego. He'd turned the wounds she inflicted into a life of beauty. Giving to the point of exhaustion.

Marla stood and cinched the sash of her russet wool coat. "I appreciate your thoughts, ladies. This has been, um, informative. But I'm on deadline. Carry on."

Back at the *Observer*, Lorraine awaited Marla's article for proofing. From there, it would travel up the ranks to Cecilia in time for Friday's circular. If this didn't read like an award-winning article … if it lacked evocative emotion … if it didn't awake sleepy citizens to get behind the Rose of Sharon, *no matter its next director* … Cecilia would never give her another shot.

She'd be relegated to writing forgettable fluff. Medical bills didn't pay themselves.

Tap, tap, tap.

"The Rose of Sharon's interim director, Sebastian Monroe, a graduate of Wild Rose Ridge High School, is quoted as saying—"

Blah. Delete.

Writing required the writer to draw from a well. Marla's well had run dry. If she continued to plug the well-spring of emotion, her story would be meaningless. Impotent ink on paper.

She shut her eyes and lifted a feeble prayer. *God, let my words achieve your purpose.*

Soon enough, words surfaced, ebbed, and flowed rhythmically. Because really, she was never limited to shallow content. Her column could easily segue to any topic that had captured her fancy and would benefit her readers and the town she represented.

As thoughts came, she typed.

> When Wild Rose Ridge found itself in desperate need of a director to replace an abruptly abandoned position at the Rose of Sharon Rescue Mission, Pastor Michael was quoted as saying, "I knew the right man to call."

Once Marla completed her assignment and the newsroom rested, readers would soon learn of Sebastian's many facets and that he'd succeeded in his goal to serve the Rose of Sharon well.

The endearing people Marla met would be encouraged to remain steadfast through difficulty. They would know what Sebastian's service and his love had taught her: God never abandons his own. He upholds them in his righteous right hand. His perfect, steady love casts out fear.

But crediting Sebastian would cost Marla the man she loved. To release him to bigger and greater things was the greatest ache.

Marla wheezed out a sigh. "What a conundrum!"

How wrong she'd been to label him unsuccessful when leaders of world organizations had clamored for his involvement.

Words could start a war, mend broken hearts, or reconcile the lost. The difference lay in how one chose to use them.

At her home office Tuesday evening, Marla word-smithed

a few sentences and tied the message with an award-winning bow.

11:59 PM. Her finger hovered over the send button with the pressure of detonating a bomb.

But first …

God, you are a good Father who's never left me. You never will. You spared my life and mended my heart. Please heal the wound I inflicted on Sebastian. Bless the work of his hands wherever you take him, and use me to make a difference in this town.

This lonely, miserable town.

The breath Marla held fell out of her lungs and emptied her like a balloon released of air. She threw herself onto her bed until exhaustion finally tugged her lids shut and enabled her mind to rest.

Friday morning's sunrise and the gift of another day kissed Marla awake.

Today her article—which had been heartily approved by Cilly—would hit the press. She whispered a prayer of gratitude that God had used Sebastian to open her eyes to see the beauty in people. To get involved in improving their lives … though it would be a hot minute before she could serve at the Rose of Sharon without missing her once upon a time secret admirer.

The scent of coffee in her kitchen and a text from Sebastian pulled Marla's feet to the floor. She popped on her reading glasses. The words came into crisp focus.

I read it.

Gulp. She typed …

Do you hate me?

I love you.

Her heart swelled.

Am I reprieved?

Yes.

Wild Rose Ridge will miss you.

Will you miss me, Marla?

Always :(Is it too late to hug you goodbye?

It's never too late.

A cleansing breath as the grey dots of Sebastian's incoming text finished dancing.

I'll meet you at the Observer.

Are we operating on Bash time?

I can't wait that long.

Mmm.

Okay :)

Marla dashed to her closet. Every shade of red bled onto the floor. How utterly monochromatic! This was no way to dress for a final goodbye.

A soothing sage green, cottony top stood out among the line-up. She tugged it on over a pair of dark jeans, filled her tumbler of coffee, and sped to work—evading Officer Huntley's radar on the way.

Outside the news building, Lorraine waved Friday's circular like a flag. "Did you see it?"

"I don't need to see it. I wrote it."

A small aircraft hummed as it passed overhead. Probably carrying Walker and Brooke on to their next big project.

And Sebastian? Soon, he'd be on his way to, well, wherever God directed him. He saw no borders and held those hunky arms open to all.

Gracious, she was going to miss those arms!

"Even you can't write a public proposal this epic."

Marla made a move to reach for the door handle. "I've had coffee. Apparently, you have not."

Blocking the door, Lorraine pursed her lips and flipped the circular Marla's direction. "Coffee isn't required to make sense of this."

Marla's gaze ran over the colored, full-page personal ad. The words shouted off the page, top to bottom.

"Marry me, Marla. Forever in love with you—Seb."

Enlarged letters, bold font. His proposition crystal clear.

"This cost him a fortune!" Marla said.

"You're worth it."

At Sebastian's familiar husky voice, Marla whirled to see him emerging from around the corner. Gaze smoky and skin tanned from hard work.

A breeze played with his hair. He wore dark canvas pants and a shirt that sported a winning shade of blue.

A small entourage of staff, volunteers, and mission residents filed up behind him. His faithful, indebted followers. A kingdom of God-fearing workers he'd established in his short time here.

Oscar, Leonard … gruff old Hilda who, yes, allowed the hint of a smile to shine behind a bulwark of seriousness.

Little Carlie and her mom.

Marla made it her practice to remember their names—all because Sebastian placed high priority on it.

Bug-eyed spectators stilled their ambling stroll outside storefronts and raised their cell phones. Murmurs kicked up.

From across the street, Barbara, Helene, Diana—chief of the matchmakers—waved arms at Lorraine, then wiggled their fingers at Marla.

A *Wild Rose Observer* mobile broadcast van pulled up adjacent to the corner.

The scenario was enough to make a skittish guy who was no friend of the media tuck tail and run. Unless Sebastian orchestrated what was shaping up to be a remarkable top story. This time, she was on the receiving end.

Quite the fuss for a goodbye hug. *Please, no.*

About that ad …

"Sebastian Monroe, you had me convinced you despise everything and everyone associated with the media, but your personal ad tells a different story."

A really romantic one.

Sebastian hadn't budged. He looked pleased with himself and in no hurry to dash out of town.

The line of spectators along Persimmon Street thickened. Fingers pointed and cameras flashed.

He advanced along the pavement, eliminating the distance. His caramel-dipped gaze moved unashamedly to her middle and held fast to her shirt.

A smile to make the moon jealous brightened his face.

She pulled at the sleeve of her shirt. "I did some sleuthing and discovered from inside sources that you're the one who had this beautiful T-shirt made."

"It fits better than I imagined."

He'd imagined her—at a time in her life when she'd let herself believe the lie that no man truly loved her and never would.

"It's a perfect shade of green," he said. "Vitality, healing, the promise of spring. Maybe second chances, if a guy is fortunate enough." He took a few more steps. "Accentuates the color of your eyes."

His words drizzled over her broken places like golden honey on a warm spring morning after an unforgiving winter. The sensation shot a voltage to her toes.

"I also had your signature in my yearbook analyzed by forensic document experts, and you know what I discovered?"

"I have rotten penmanship."

"Definitely."

His shoulders shook in a laugh.

"You're the one who wrote those cards during my treatments."

A pink tinge blossomed on his cheeks. His throat bobbed like a kid caught making out.

"After some digging, I read dozens of testimonies from people who credit you for enriching their lives. A YouTube video detailed a cast of grateful people you encountered after Hurricane Helene devastated western North Carolina."

He pursed his lips and nodded.

"A woman in Bangladesh reported about a long-haired angel who performed CPR on her son after their house collapsed. Said angel spared the boy's life, found temporary housing for them while garnering the muscle of local villagers to rebuild her home. She said the man refused to give his name but blessed her in the name of Jesus. These and other reports are all Hallmark Sebastian encounters."

Give it up for her meddling capabilities that worked in her favor.

"I don't have a degree in English lit like you do, but I believe the meaning in my ad is clear."

Right, that.

His gaze bloomed with intention. Not one of those gloriously lean, strident muscles in his body wavered. He well knew she could publicly humiliate him again in front of a growing crowd.

Despite the way she'd crushed him, he'd stayed steady in her rocky and lonely life all along, loving from safe distance. He was blind to the ugliness of her scars.

"I have great respect for you and the work you've done, Seb. I'm an idiot to have missed how wonderful you are when I had the chance. How can you not hate me for what I did?"

"That's what forgiveness is for."

Heads bobbed all around. A shower of whoops, crouching videographers, and flash of cameras accompanied their banter.

"I love you, Marla. My heart is yours if you want it."

Endless possibilities opened up and broke the barriers

of small town media where she'd been hiding a lonely, wounded heart behind her weekly byline.

The sensation of floating lifted her heels from the ground.

"I get extreme anxiety on airplanes and seasick in a bathtub, but I'm willing to serve alongside you wherever you go."

"I'm not going anywhere."

Eliminating the distance, Sebastian grasped her hands and squeezed. "There's no end to the needs everywhere. But God has called me to serve in this location. Close to you."

A tremor shuddered through her body. Water stung her eyes, blurring his face.

What a rare jewel!

She drew an interlaced hand to his chest, felt the drumming.

"Someone in classifieds should be fired for omitting the, uh, question mark at the end of your ad."

A provocative smile blossomed in Sebastian's gaze and curled the edge of his mouth. "I'm not asking a question."

"Semantics."

"Bottom line, I'm not letting you out of my sight."

"May I quote you?"

He unleashed a laugh that fanned the heat in her body to an inferno. Then, ever so slowly, Sebastian lowered to one knee.

An achy longing pooled in his gentle gaze. "Marry me, Marla."

With one hand, she palmed his cheek as though he were sculpted of Italian marble on display in the Louvre.

"Sebastian Monroe, angel of the Ridge, that's a resounding yes."

Agily, he returned to his feet and kissed her so possessively she lost all sense of time and space.

After what felt like years, he broke their kisses. "News this great really should be put on record."

"Definitely quoting you."

Sebastian unleashed a newsworthy smile and drew her to himself. "I'd be hurt if you didn't."

Bedazzled and breathless, Marla closed the book on her own happy ending with the real life hero whose heart was hers to have and to hold all along.

The Article

THE WILD ROSE OBSERVER

M**arla Mavis, senior staff writer**

When Wild Rose Ridge found itself in desperate need of a director to replace an abruptly abandoned position at the Rose of Sharon Rescue Mission, Pastor Michael was quoted as saying, "I knew the right man to call."

Pastor Michael isn't the only one who's become a believer in that right man.

Humanitarian Sebastian Monroe*, a former citizen of the Ridge, didn't hesitate to accept the opportunity.

What was intended to be a human interest piece took a hard left in the process of gathering research. Because the Rose of Sharon was not designed to operate under the authority of one.

Parsed down to its simplest explanation, there was a need. Sebastian rose to meet it.

But without the countless souls who have sacrificed time, talent, and resources to make it run, many in our area are without hope.

For the guests who've passed through the door, the mission offers more than a meal. It offers a heart that is full.

The compound showcases what can be accomplished through those who are willing to serve where they are uncomfortable. It means being involved in things that history will gladly tell of for years to come.

Organizations such as the one we are privileged to support in Wild Rose Ridge are a gateway to the transcendent. They connect us to a purpose that is far grander than ourselves.

To many, the Ridge is known for tourism, commerce, quaint small town charm, neighborly vibes, historic preservation, stunning panorama, and long-standing traditions. But the crown jewel isn't any one individual. Rather, it's the collective of humanity—those who live and work and serve here.

The body is made up of many parts. One person wasn't designed to sustain the Rose of Sharon alone, no matter how industrious and capable those hands may be. Some residents have gone on and left an impact we are enjoying today.

What legacy will each of us leave? Are we doing everything we can with the resources, talents, and time we've been given?

What part will you play so that others will know hope?

*Monroe was opposed to having his name associated with the article, but the evidence of his involvement is undeniable in the lives of those who've been blessed to know him.

Dear Reader

Thanks for reading **Marry Me, Marla**, my capstone ending to the Wild Rose Ridge contemporary series!

As secondary characters are apt to do, this red-wigged, nosy … or, shall I say, duly inquisitive … reporter of my four previous books had her own story to tell.

So, how to create Marla Mavis as a relatable, sympathetic protagonist? Give her a health scare, a heartbreak, and a humanitarian hero who secretly loves her.

Reviews are golden! Please share your brief, kind, and honest thoughts on Amazon, Goodreads, and/or Bookbub and help **Marry Me, Marla** find its way to other romance readers.

Prequel, This I Promise You

In **Marry Me, Marla**, Marla references Chef Bryan J. Carlyle and his wife Adelyn. Their second chance, jilted bride romance—and the powerful story behind the name Ben's Seafood and Grille—is told in the award-winning prequel to the Heart of Moreland Manor Series.

This happy couple fought hard to overcome betrayal and rejection to find their way back to the altar.

Enjoy this excerpt from **This I Promise You** …

Say the name Bryan J. Carlyle and women swooned. Yes, a well-loved celebrity chef, proprietor of one of New Orleans' three-star Michelin restaurants, and charming cooking show host who sported broad shoulders and endearing eyes.

But it wasn't their hearts he'd ravaged at the altar.

If Ruthie, one of Adelyn Ormond's fifth-grade students at Leon Anthony Elementary School, hadn't served up a sweet, Monday morning smile, Adelyn might have collapsed into one of the lunchroom chairs.

"You want me to do *what*?" She restrained her tone with effort, the smell of today's menu—corn dogs, green peas, and milk—souring her stomach.

"Keep your voice down. You're causing the students undue concern."

Adelyn finger-waved at Ruthie before turning back to her task-driven supervisor, Principal Katherine McClellan who, clearly, had lost her marbles.

"It's merely one afternoon, Adelyn."

"One afternoon with ... him."

Despite years of ballet training, she struggled to assume proper posture in the wake of an assignment that all but turned her core to rubber.

Katherine stooped to folding her arms, cocked a head. "The School Board's decision to ask you to secure a high-profile individual to support this year's Second Harvest fundraiser was not taken lightly."

"Bryan is not some random high-profile person."

"... the same group that believed your philanthropic stance was worthy of their unanimous nomination for the district's Teacher of the Year."

A prestigious award Adelyn had achieved last year due

to her interaction with education stakeholders which resulted in their school being a recipient of the backpack program to feed underserved students.

Twisting screws now. "And you well know the only decent meal some of our students receive comes by way of Second Harvest's provisions."

"I'm more than happy to be spearheading the event and have established a rock-solid planning committee. I'm the proverbial poster child to support causes like this. It's about the *chef*."

"We're sympathetic to your situation, Adelyn, but that was six months ago."

"Situation? It was a catastrophe. You don't derail a woman's life—her dream wedding—in front of five hundred people and expect her to just—"

"The board has simply asked you to extend a personal invitation to Chef Carlyle to participate ... being that you know him."

She blinked at her. "Know him? I wore his ring, for heaven's sake. But it's not like we're best pals. Not anymore anyway ..."

A cold chill pricked at her skin. Her gaze drifted over the sea of chattering students. "At least not in the truest sense of the word where two people share mutual trust, talk over a burger and fries." Or Bryan's wholly unique grilled chicken sandwich with fennel-basil slaw on a toasted brioche bun.

A tapestry of fragrances niggled into her memory. She shirked them off—along with the delicious feel of his wink when he'd slid the plated sandwich her direction.

"The man eviscerated me, Katherine. Made me the laughingstock of the entire ... *cuisine* community."

"His reason for leaving you at the altar does beg explanation." Katherine jagged a brow. "But that photo of you was, uh, quite incriminating. Perhaps when you contact him it would provide an opportunity for you to—"

"Find someone else to ask for Chef Carlyle's involvement. And since he is loved the world over, this won't be difficult." She lifted her hand to cute Tate Samson, coaxed a smile.

"He will agree if you are involved."

The bell screamed through the lunchroom.

Adelyn froze. "What?"

"Jeanette has already called his publicity agent. Bordered on begging."

"The assistant principal is involved in this fiasco?"

"It was suggested that he'd attend the event and consider a cooking demo if you were his sous-chef, working alongside him."

The walls closed in. She gave her head a slow shake and huffed.

"What's it going to be, Adelyn? Let the children starve?"

Ruthie's question out on the playground during recess wrapped Adelyn's lungs in a gauze of end-stage summer heat.

"When's your birthday, Miss Ormond?"

"March. Six months ago."

"Whadya get?"

Jilted.

The hyped-up social event of Adelyn and Bryan's wedding promised to deliver the highly anticipated vow exchange between Chef Bryan J. Carlyle and his sweetheart. Only they'd witnessed her ... left alone in a custom gown, her rose and gardenia bouquet wilted by tears.

"I got surprises, Ruthie," Adelyn finally said, releasing a breath she'd been holding.

For some, painful surprises were the stuff of birthdays.

"My daddy said he'd give me a bicycle for my birthday."

Confidence oozed in Ruthie's voice. *Dear God, make that dad keep his promise.*

Tempering a fresh wave of irritation, Adelyn took the box of vanilla cupcakes swirled in pink and bright green frosting and called her students to gather around a nearby picnic table.

Tate pinned a gaze on the box. "What's the cupcakes for, Miss Ormond?"

Adelyn moved a pointed finger across the increasingly curious expressions. "I special ordered these from The Pear Tree bakery to celebrate my amazing students and the start of a new and successful year."

Judging from the toothy—and not so toothy—nine and ten-year-old smiles, her affirmation had achieved its purpose. But sometimes disappointment hid behind the veneer of a smile.

She lit each of the twisted white candles cemented in a dome of cheery frosting. The vacant stares suggested they were unaccustomed to being celebrated, not a one of them itching to blow out the rapidly melting candles.

Teaching gave her an opportunity to be a voice of truth

in a child's life. To ensure they heard what they might not hear otherwise ... that they were precious in the eyes of God and worth a promise kept.

Some girls being the exception.

She extinguished the flickering flames with a hard puff, plated and distributed the cupcakes.

"Listen up, Team Ormond." *Should have been Carlyle.* "Take time to enjoy a cupcake and listen for my call to line up in about fifteen minutes."

Most students remained seated. A few abandoned their cupcake after a few bites and scattered to various areas within the playground.

A breeze rippled over the table and carried a pink party napkin to the chain-link fence encasing the playground. Following it, Adelyn's gaze landed on her student Jace Murray.

Sitting alone with his back to the fence.

A thin boy with baggy shorts and oversized Commanders T-shirt bearing the same grass stain she'd noticed yesterday … and the day before that.

Last week, too?

The agonizing minutes she'd spent this morning getting ready for work, fussing over which of many outfits coordinated best with her latest shoe purchase accosted her conscience

When their eyes met, Jace hugged his knees to his chest and lagged a glance away. Sunlight played on his gaunt face, shadows pooling in his sunken cheeks.

Seven cupcakes remained. No doubt Mom and Adelyn's stepdad—Henry James Russell—would appreciate them. But their pantry held plenty of food.

Box in hand, Adelyn crossed over to Jace and sat beside him.

He didn't flinch.

"Did you catch my technique, Jace? Darn near extinguished every one of those candles in one breath."

He shook his head with the enthusiasm of a kid offered a make-up tutorial. But food? That brought people together.

Raising the lid, she released the sweet redolence of custom bakery and moved the box near his nose. "My guess is you're a lime green frosting kind of guy."

Jace worked a mean mug into his profile, refusing eye contact. A stomach growl betrayed his attempt to remain disinterested.

"C'mon, help me out. It's been an epic challenge to recover my ballet body."

A challenge brought on by recklessly eating herself into a coma on occasion, an attempt to feel nothing of the barbs from having lost her happily ever after.

One cheek hitched. "Dancing. Guess that's why you so slim, Miss Ormond."

Crystalline sugar chilled her cheeks as she bit into a pink-frosted cupcake, an indulgence she'd often denied herself when she danced professionally. And the need to keep fit for a wedding gown had ended. Abruptly.

Jace grabbed a stick near his feet, tossed it. "You don't got nothing to worry about."

His profile hid the hint of amusement before his expression returned to a solemn state.

Sunlight emerged from behind a curtain of parting clouds and targeted the softened frosting. Recess ended in a few minutes … tick, tick, tick.

Lord, help me make a heart connection.

"Ballet isn't for sissies, you know."

"Why'd you give up dancing?"

"I had an injury that forced my retirement. A friend I'd danced with in Pacific Northwest Ballet left her career to open a dance studio in Wild Rose Ridge, Washington, and she asked if I'd teach a few classes. The experience inspired me to get a degree in elementary education. The only difference now is my students aren't required to wear leotards and tights."

His chest chugged in a minimal laugh, dimples more apparent.

"Why'd you come to Louisiana?"

"I moved here to be closer to my parents."

Information enough for a ten-year old.

Because, yes, she'd broken things off with possessive boyfriend Davis Coleman, a running back for the Seattle Seahawks, but the pivotal reason she relocated was Dad's teary confession that Mom's dementia had become more pronounced.

With increasing frequency, Mom had misplaced things. Among them, Dad's leather pouch that held a prized military service medal. Days later, he'd found it tucked away in his chest of drawers. Only it wasn't the pouch. It was Dad's wallet, put there for safe keeping, Mom had explained.

"Just think, if God hadn't led me to Louisiana, I'd never have met you."

Adelyn hadn't achieved Teacher of the Year for no reason. The title held the weighty responsibility to affirm impressionable souls. Because one affirmation spoken to one soul who'd received it could change their life forever

—just as a broken promise could part a girl's head from her heart.

He fisted and flung a stone, the projectile smacking the metal swing set yards away.

"The Commanders could use a QB with your skill."

That drew a smile.

"We've got three more minutes before recess ends." She raised the box of cupcakes again, hitched her brows in exaggerated invitation. "Save the day, please?"

At that, Jace sank his teeth into a lime green cupcake, taking wolfish bites as if this were his last meal.

"Hungry, are we?"

His dull expression held palpable seriousness. Hunger no laughing matter, it seemed. A daily struggle.

"There's not really enough to go around at home, ya know?"

In fact, she did.

Hunger visited Adelyn and her brother Ken when Rex Ormond gambled away his meager earnings and spent the winnings on the companionship of hard drink.

Just you wait and see, Addie girl. I promise you this time I'm gonna hit paydirt.

At the chime of a nearby church, Adelyn wrestled free from memory's grip.

What would it mean to Jace and his family if they no longer faced scarcity? What good was sharing Jesus's love if Adelyn didn't demonstrate how it looked on a functional level? Claiming to have faith without deeds didn't achieve faith's highest purpose.

Adelyn stood. "I'm sending the rest of these cupcakes home with you."

The resistant stare quickly faded to a pleading gaze. He

snatched the box like she'd offered him gold coins. She bet Jace wouldn't eat any of the meager offering until his family ate first.

A warm breeze kicked up dust. Her students continued to swing, run around, and release happy squeals.

She cupped a hand to her mouth. "Let's go, children. Recess is over."

They scrambled to form a line in front of her on the walkway along the side entrance. Jace tucked the sacred pastry box under his arm like a running back, daring anyone to pop the ball loose.

Angst tugged at her heart and fisted in her middle. If Chef Extraordinaire could not be convinced to contribute to a good cause, Jace and numerous others like him might remain food insecure.

Involving Bryan would required supreme sacrifice. But it would not come by way of adding one more feather to his already heavily feathered cap. She'd only consent to the idiocy because, providentially, she'd been made aware of Jace's need.

Tiny fissures developed in relationships marked by broken promises. Over time, they became unnavigable chasms. But a promise kept nourished the soul and conveyed something about the promise maker.

Would a collaboration with Carlyle the Creep stir a willingness to hear his side of the story? Was there a sinister secret behind his struggle to discuss his family? What would be the outcome if they made the giant leap to lay everything out in the open? And would it offer any hope of rekindling their relationship?

Pfft. Hopeless.

If only public humiliation was just cause for torching a guy's restaurant.

At some point Bryan J. Carlyle would find the gumption to delete the hazy image of Adelyn—his ex-fiancée—lip-locked with some unfamiliar jerk. Few things were more intolerable than mischaracterization, and deceit was a poison he refused to drink. For now, upholding the status of his cooking show ratings required his undivided attention.

Or so said Trent Barks, his publicity manager who—aptly named—doubled as Bryan's conscience.

The floor-to-ceiling windows in Trent's fourth-floor office framed the Monday afternoon sun as it climbed above the west end of the French Quarter and made an oven of an otherwise amply air-conditioned space.

Morphing into the posture of Judge Judy, Trent sat stiffly in his chair, his hands clasped atop his desk.

Bryan squirmed beneath a white-hot stare. "My ratings can't be down. They've done nothing but climb since I agreed to this cooking show gig a year ago. Fans are wild about *Carlyle's Cookin' Something Up.*"

Bryan's cell buzzed within the patch pocket of his double-breasted chef's coat. Unknown caller? He silenced his cell and slipped it back inside the pocket.

"You don't pay me to spread sunshine, Bryan. I'm merely giving you the facts. And the fact is, Don Juan, following your hasty exit at the altar last March, you've got to redirect the course of your reputation, or it's gonna sink to a watery grave of first-season flops."

"I'm ranked sixth among leading executive chefs in New Orleans, and I'm in the top ten list of celebrity chefs people most wish to have cook for them. Locals rate Ben's Seafood and Grille as their prime choice with a demand to open a restaurant in the Pacific Northwest." He raised a finger. "*Aaaand* I've got the cooking school."

Taking generous investment capital from stock market earnings, he'd opened Carlyle's Cooking School five years ago. Patrons worldwide had enjoyed the expansive, front-end retail shop and backroom cooking demos that hosted a wide variety of groups.

"One bold move isn't going to take me down, Trent."

Save the family tragedy.

"True. But like all good things—"

With an upturned palm, Bryan intercepted Trent's negativity before it slammed into his soul like a Gulf Coast Cat 5 hurricane. "I owe the success of my enterprises to God. I can't see why he'd allow what happened between me and Adelyn to destroy it."

Any venture that brought people around the family table would have his full support and ingenuity. Especially if it gave them what he'd lost.

"Trent, you've always said I'm the guy who can make mud pies that have people eating out of my hands."

"Which has worked in your favor until now. I suggest you layer on the charm when you're at the studio. Keep yourself lovable."

"Bolstering a reputation isn't a recipe a guy follows, controlling the process to ensure perfect results."

"Garnering artificial adoration is better than nothing."

Was it?

Trent set his feet on the desk, clasped hands behind his head, his tone remarkably whimsical. "Thanks to my persuasion, the media has touted you as the people's chef —the guy with a winning smile and signature double-breasted chef's coat who folds the collar down like a crisp linen napkin."

"None of that matters without stage presence and cooking savvy."

"You do draw people like flies to honey. Beats the heck out of me why you haven't already put a ring on some other girl's finger."

"Listen, Trent, you stick to managing the publicity, and I'll manage my love life."

"What love life, BJ? I say you leave the past alone and turn to greener pastures."

Other women had vied for Bryan's attention, but Adelyn had captured the entirety of his heart, mind, and soul when they met at Deutsches Haus Oktoberfest.

"If we're done here—"

Trent balled a fist in his palm. "Your social media has become a feeding frenzy, fodder for gossip columnists who aren't jazzed you led a decent girl to the altar and left her there."

"It was justified."

If only those columnists and the viewing world knew the reason. The desire for vindication still simmered beneath his skin. Truth was, he still cared for Adelyn, though, by all appearances, she'd been unfaithful. Stupid him. He presumed theirs was an unquenchable love … the kind that'd drawn him to his knees—for the first time—to offer her his heart in marriage.

Because marriage was forever.

Adelyn's beautiful image appeared in his mind, rising like a delicate vapor over a cup of gumbo, and tantalized his senses. He grasped at it then …

"I can't marry someone I don't trust, Adelyn!"

Her deer in headlights, ashen face, and wringing hands clipped his 'until death parts us' promise like high-grade kitchen shears.

Snap, snap. "Earth to BJ."

The light of Trent's computer screen highlighted furrows across his stormy brow. "Believe what you will on the personal end, Bryan. As for business, you—the magnificent curator of fresh produce and herbs—should know that all good growth dies unless properly tended."

An incoming call. The same unfamiliar number.

"If that's opportunity calling, BJ, you'd better pick up."

Bryan jingled the keys to his Jag and turned at the door. "You just do what you're paid to do, and trust me to work magic."

Please, trust me.

Acknowledgments

Susan May Warren, scene feedback.

Pattie Frampton, craft partner and fellow-connoisseur of a satisfying romance.

My MBT (My Book Therapy) author Huddle: Alyssa Schwarz, Kathy Geary Anderson, Linda Jo Reed, Dalyn Weller, and Kit Morgan.

Beta readers, Dr. Margaret A. Eomurian and Kathy Geary Anderson.

Amy Petrowich, consistency reader, editor.

Mary Anne Rhyne Vanderburg, proofreader and Communications Consultant for WordHive.

Heather Wilbur, map design.

Erin Dameron-Hill, cover artist. (https://www.edhprofessionals.com)

Books by Mary

Wild Rose Ridge Series
A Steel Rose
One Starry Christmas
By Summer's End
Fall for Me
Marry Me, Marla
♡
Love in Laurelton Series
Call to Love, Book 1
Available in hardback, (Pelican Book Group) Kindle & Audible
♡
The Heart of Moreland Manor Series
This I Promise You, Prequel*
[*This award-winning ebook is FREE to new subscribers @ maryfelkins.com]
You Are the Reason, Book 1
Sweeter with You, Book 2
When You Smile For Me, Book 3

♡

Devotional

What The Morning Brings: 52 Story-Style Devotions

Find all Felkins fiction and blog posts @ maryfelkins.com

About the Author

Mary A. Felkins is a multi-published, award-winning author of closed door romance whose novels deliver no shortage of sizzle, sass, and passion. She is a blogger and a member of ACFW, My Book Therapy, Novel Academy, and FHLCW. (Faith Hope and Love Christian Writers)

She can be lured from her creative writing space if presented with an unopened bag of Peanut M&Ms. A surprise appearance by her teen idol, Donny Osmond, would also do the trick—although she'd likely pass out.

If she likes your first or last name, expect it to show up in one of her novels.

To receive Mary's author newsletters with social and exclusive author updates, subscribe via email at www.-maryfelkins.com. FREE novella to new subscribers!